HANDBOOK OF VANCE SPACE

HANDBOOK of VANCE SPACE

Everyman's Guide to the Planets of the
Alastor Cluster, the Gaean Reach,
the Oikumene, and other exotic sectors
from the Science Fiction of Jack Vance

MICHAEL ANDRE-DRIUSSI

SIRIUS FICTION Albany, California

Front cover image © Piotr Krzeslak/Shutterstock

First edition: 2014

Hardcover ISBN: 978-0-9642795-6-8
Paperback ISBN: 978-0-9642795-7-5

Sirius Fiction
P.O. Box 6248
Albany, CA 94706

CONTENTS

ABBREVIATIONS

Note on form of citation: "(DM 12)" means "*The Dragon Masters,* chapter twelve."

AbS   "Abercrombie Station" (Monsters in Orbit 1)

AC   "Assault on a City," also known as "The Insufferable Red-haired Daughter of Commander Tynnot, O.T.E."

An   *The Anome* (Durdane I), also known as *The Faceless Man*

ArS   *Araminta Station* (Cadwal I)

As   *The Asutra* (Durdane III)

BD   *The Book of Dreams* (Demon Princes V)

BFM   *The Brave Free Men* (Durdane II)

BP   *Big Planet*

BW   *The Blue World*

CAD   The Cadwal Chronicles series

CC   *City of the Chasch* (Tschai I), also known as *The Chasch*

CG   "Coup de Grâce" (Magnus Ridolph 10), also known as "Worlds of Origin"

CHO   "Cholwell's Chickens" (Monsters in Orbit 2)

CM   "Crusade to Maxus," also known as "Overlords of Maxus"

D   *The Dirdir* (Tschai III)

DM   *The Dragon Masters*

DP   The Demon Princes series

DSB   "The Devil on Salvation Bluff"

DTA   "The Dogtown Tourist Agency" (Galactic Effectuator 1)

DU   The Durdane trilogy

E	*Emphyrio*
EOE	*Ecce and Old Earth* (Cadwal II)
F	*The Face* (Demon Princes IV)
FGB	*The Five Gold Bands,* also known as *The Rapparee*
FT	"Freitzke's Turn" (Galactic Effectuator 2)
GAB	"The Gift of Gab"
GI	*Gold and Iron,* also known as *Slaves of the Klau*
GOG	"Golden Girl"
GPr	*The Gray Prince,* also known as *The Domains of Koryphon*
HB	"The Howling Bounders" (Magnus Ridolph 7)
HI	*The Houses of Iszm*
HL	"The House Lords"
HLD	"Hard Luck Diggings" (Magnus Ridolph 1)
KM	*The Killing Machine* (Demon Princes II)
KT	"The King of Thieves" (Magnus Ridolph 5)
KW	"The Kokod Warriors" (Magnus Ridolph 9)
LC	*The Last Castle*
LP	*The Languages of Pao*
Lu	*Lurulu* (Ports of Call II)
l.y.	light-year (a unit of interstellar distance)
Ma	*Marune: Alastor 933*
MD	"Masquerade on Dicantropus"
MM	"The Moon Moth"
MMU	"Meet Miss Universe"
MT	*Maske: Thaery*
MW	"The Miracle Workers"
MZ	"The Man from Zodiac," also known as "Milton Hack from Zodiac"
NeP	"The New Prime," also known as "Brain of the Galaxy"
NL	*Night Lamp*
NOP	"Nopalgarth," also known as "The Brains of Earth"
PBD	"Planet of the Black Dust"
PF	"Phalid's Fate"
PL	*The Palace of Love* (Demon Princes III)
Pn	*The Pnume* (Tschai IV)
POC	*Ports of Call*

POT	"The Potters of Firsk"
SAN	"Sanatoris Short-cut" (Magnus Ridolph 2)
ShW	*Showboat World* (Big Planet II) also known as *The Magnificent Showboats of the Lower Vissel River, Lune XXIII South, Big Planet*
SJA	"Sjambak"
SK	*Star King* (Demon Princes I)
SO	*Space Opera*
SPA	"The Spa of the Stars" (Magnus Ridolph 8)
SSP	"Sabotage on Sulfur Planet"
SSS	"The Sub-Standard Sardines" (Magnus Ridolph 3)
ST	*Son of the Tree*
SU	"Shape-Up"
SuP	"Sulwen's Planet"
SvW	*Servants of the Wankh* (Tschai II) also known as *The Wannek*
TB	"Men of the Ten Books," also known as "The Ten Books"
TEM	"The Temple of Han," also known as "The God and the Temple Robber"
Th	*Throy* (Cadwal III)
TLF	*To Live Forever,* also known as *Clarges*
TLJ	"Three-legged Joe"
TOB	"To B or Not to C or to D" (Magnus Ridolph 6), also known as "Cosmic Hotfoot"
Tr	*Trullion: Alastor 2262*
UM	"The Unspeakable McInch" (Magnus Ridolph 4)
UR	"Ullward's Retreat"
W	*Wyst: Alastor 1716*
WB	"The World Between," also known as "Ecological Onslaught"
WFM	"When the Five Moons Rise"
WLA	"Winner Lose All," also known as "The Visitors"
WT	"The World Thinker"

Novels: 31

Short Novels: 2

Novellas: 8

Novelettes: 17

Short Stories: 19

THE "CAESAR CIPHER"

There are a number of points in this handbook where information of a particularly sensitive matter is given under the cover of the Caesar Cipher.

CIPHER	A	B	C	D	E	F	G	H	I	J	K	L	M
Plain	d	e	f	g	h	i	j	k	l	m	n	o	p

CIPHER	N	O	P	Q	R	S	T	U	V	W	X	Y	Z
Plain	q	r	s	t	u	v	w	x	y	z	a	b	c

ACKNOWLEDGEMENTS

Special thanks go to the following for their help:

Dan'l Danehy-Oakes looked over the manuscript and provided many useful comments.

Dave Langford gave copious notes on the earlier chapbook form.

Gordon Brain pressed for Iszm, Kyril, Pangborn, and others.

Andrew Joron gave important star catalogue index research early on.

David Granvold rescued the box of books when I went away, and years later gave it back to me. True friend!

INDEX OF ENTRIES

Arcturus / 10
Arcturus Legend / 10
Ardemizian / 10
Argo Navis / 10
Argo Navis
   14-AR-366 / 10
Argo Navis 961 / 10

Aries 44R951 / 10
Aries Sector / 10
Arneb / 10
Aspergill / 10
Aspidiske / 11
Atreus / 11
Aume / 11

Auriga 225-G / 11
Auriol / 11
Avente / 11
Axelbarren / 11
Azul / 11
Azulias / 11

B

Badau / 11
Bakaima / 11
Baliberos / 12
Ballen / 12
Ballenkarch / 12
Balmath / 12
Banacre / 12
Bao / 12
Barleycorn / 12
Baten Kaitos / 12
Batmarsh / 12
Beau Aire / 12
Beland / 12
Bella's Pride / 12
Bellatrix V / 12

Belotsi / 12
Bernal / 13
Bethune Preserve / 13
Beyond / 13
BGD 1169 / 14
Bhutra / 14
Big Planet / 14
Bissom's End / 15
Bista / 15
Blaise / 15
Blanche / 15
Blazon / 15
Blenkinsop,
   Moulder 17 / 15
Blue-eyed Devil / 16

Blue Planet / 16
Blue-star / 16
Blue Star / 16
Blue World / 16
Bogardus / 18
Boniface / 18
Bossom's World / 19
Bran / 19
Breakness / 19
Brengastel / 19
Brinktown / 19
Bruse-Tansel / 19
Bugtown / 19

C

Cadwal / 20
Caffin's World / 21
Cairre / 21
Calbys / 21
Camberwell / 21
Cambiasq / 22
Cambyses / 22
Canopus / 22

Capella / 22
Caph / 22
Carina 4269 / 23
Carina LO-461 / 23
Carnegie Twelve / 23
Caro / 23
Cassiopeia 993:9 / 23
Castlegran / 23

Cepheus 9621 / 23
Cestus FQR910 / 23
Ceti 1620 / 23
Chamanita Planet / 23
Chandaria / 23
Chankozar / 23
Channel Planet / 24
Chastain / 24

D

E

L

M

N

O

P

TABLES AND MAPS

ENTRIES

 Entries marked with flag symbol indicate Star Governments.

NUMERIC ENTRIES

1012 AURIGAE home star system of the intelligent Golespods, wide, rubbery creatures (UM).

1109TH CLUSTER an area of the Milky Way galaxy where local cultures are decadent (NeP).

A

ACHERNAR Alpha Eridani (MMU). Alien inhabited system, where a representative autochthon looks like a green-scaled armadillo with a wasp head. This species is highly telepathic. "Achernar" is a real name for the star, which is located 139 l.y. from Old Earth.

ADHIL star of planet Loristan in constellation Andromeda (FGB 5). Historically this name has been applied to many stars in Andromeda:
1. Xi Andromedae, a K0 III (giant) star located 214 l.y. from Old Earth.
2. 60 Andromedae, a K3.5 III (giant) star located 530 l.y. from Old Earth.
3. 49 Andromedae.
4. Chi Andromedae, a G8 III (giant) star located 250 l.y. from Old Earth.

AERLITH a planet of star Skene, in a star cluster, location unknown (DM).

An Earth-like world with a sidereal day of 144 hours. Coralyne, the home star of the Basics (or home planet, there being some ambiguity), swings by periodically, at which time a wave of Basics invades Aerlith.

POPULATION:

- *Colonists:* Humans (called Utter Men by the sacerdotes).
- *Invaders:* Basics or "grephs" (reptilian humanoids).
- *Autochthons:* Sacerdotes (subterranean people, golden-haired, always naked).

GOVERNMENT: Balkanized into petty principalities.

TECHNOLOGY: Early gunpowder (pistols, blunderbusses) except for advanced bioengineering techniques stolen from the Basics which allow the humans to craft a wide variety of "dragon" fighting beasts from captured Basics. (The Basics use this same technique to create "warriors" from modified human stock.)

HUMAN-BRED DRAGONS (BY TYPE)

Name	Notes
Spider	The mount ridden by humans.
Termagant	A footsoldier equally adept with lance, cutlass, mace, and pistol.
Long-horned Murderer	This seems to be a heavy cavalry creature.
Striding Murderer	This seems to be a light cavalry creature.
Blue Horror	This creature has pinchers.
Fiend	This creature uses sword and mace, but it also has a tail with a heavy spiked ball. Good against Juggers.
Jugger	The biggest creature, elephantine. It is capable of using handweapons, but also able to rip enemies in half with its hands.

GREPH-BRED WARRIORS (BY TYPE)

Name	Notes
Mount	Ridden by Basics, it hops like a rabbit.
Heavy Trooper	An armored footsoldier with blaster, sword, etc.
Weaponeer	A soldier armed with advanced energy weapons on swivels.
Tracker	A scout capable of tracking by scent, and good at climbing.
Giant	Twice the size of a man, armed with a blaster, and wearing armor.

Planet Aerlith

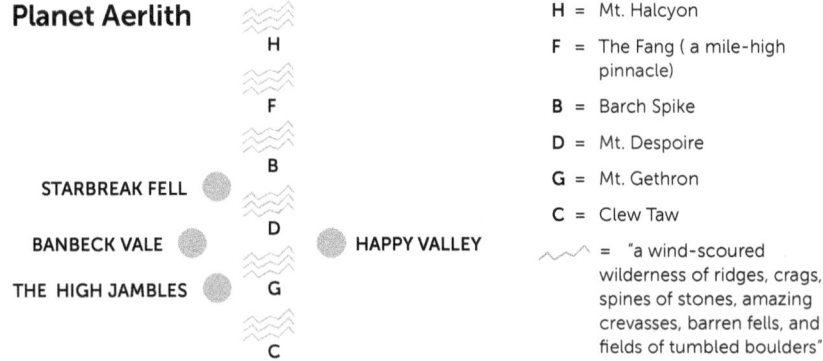

STARBREAK FELL

BANBECK VALE

THE HIGH JAMBLES

HAPPY VALLEY

H = Mt. Halcyon
F = The Fang (a mile-high pinnacle)
B = Barch Spike
D = Mt. Despoire
G = Mt. Gethron
C = Clew Taw
~~~ = "a wind-scoured wilderness of ridges, crags, spines of stones, amazing crevasses, barren fells, and fields of tumbled boulders"

ARTS: The tand, the amulet fetish of the sacerdote.

HISTORY: Humans came to Aerlith as exiles during War of the Ten Stars; the Nightmare Coalition apparently defeated the Old Rule, also known as the Human Empire (DM 4). There is talk of Earth, Eden, and Tempe being names for the planet of ultimate human origin (DM 12).

HISTORY OF AERLITH

Years Ago	Event
812	Sacerdotes begin YRFIAFKD QEBFO PQXOPEFM RKABODOLRKA.
300?	Happy Valley dominant, arrival of the grephs.
275?	Age of Wet Iron.
270?	After 5 years of peace, the return of the grephs.

AEVIR an inhabited world (NeP).

AKHABATS the planet where Langtry star-drives are assembled by the Sons of Langtry (FGB 1). Its star is Prosperus.

ALASEN an orange star, one eye of Gorcula the Dragonfish (BFM 6).

ALASTOR 458 see PHARIS.

ALASTOR 485 see ELLENT.

ALASTOR 503 see ZECK.

ALASTOR 933 see MARUNE.

ALASTOR 965 see RHAMNOTIS.

ALASTOR 1102 see BRUSE-TANSEL.

ALASTOR 1317 see TSAMBARA.

ALASTOR 1716 see WYST.

ALASTOR 1740 see GRAY WORLD.

ALASTOR 2121 see DEULLE.

ALASTOR 2262 see TRULLION.

ALASTOR CLUSTER 🚩 contemporary to the Gaean Reach, the Alastor Cluster is an interstellar nation 20 to 30 light years across, containing 3,000 worlds ruled from planet Numenes by the Connatic and his space navy, the Whelm. Said to be "out toward the rim" from Old Earth (Tr 1), the cluster is bounded by the Unfortunate Waste, the Nonestic Gulf, and the Gaean Reach to one side, the Darkling Regions, the Primarchic, the Rubrimar Cluster, the Erdic Sector, and the Primarchic to the other (Tr prologue; W 3). (The name "Alastor" itself is from Greek mythology: the avenging demon who visits the sins of the fathers on their children.)

The Alastor Cluster is divided up into twenty-three realms, each nominally ruled by one of twenty-three goddesses, including Cassadense, Corë of the Four Bosoms, Giampara, and Thaia (W glossary). Each inhabited world has a Cursar, a representative of the Connatic, usually located in an enclave known as "Alastor Centrality" (W 1). By ancient custom, the Connatic roams anonymously throughout the cluster.

Commonly named constellations based upon the Cluster's internal structure include: Fiamifer, the Crystal Eel, Koon's Hole, the Goodby Place (W 2). Cluster currency is the "ozol," equivalent to the Gaean SVU (the "dinket" is a coin worth one-tenth of an ozol; 100-ozol notes are red and black).

For individual planets, see Arcady, Azulias, Balmath, Blazon, Bruse-Tansel, Deulle, Ellent, Gray World, Green Star, Illucante, Imber, Kandaspe, Maranian, Marune, Numenes, Pharis, Rhamnotis, Rufous Planet, Triskelion, Trullion, Tsambara, Wyst, Xampias, and Zeck.

USEFUL TERMS:

Hassade—a popular team sport; see "Appendix II: Sports."

Naaetic art—that critique concerned with the awe, beauty, and grandeur associated with space ships.

ALBIREO VII the homeworld of the Phanes is a moon of this planet (LC 4). "Albireo" is an old name for Beta Cygni, lying 430 l.y. from Old Earth.

ALCANTARA an inhabited world (E 31).

ALCIDE a world of the Gaean Reach (GPr 1).

ALCYDON a world of the Gaean Reach (POC 7.1).

ALCYONE star, also known as Eta Tauri, 370 l.y. from Old Earth (BD 4).

ALEXANDER a world with a yellow sea (WLA).

ALGENIB star, also known as Gamma Pegasi, 390 l.y. from Old Earth.
- *Algenib IV*—Clarendon, an inhabited world of the Gaean Reach (EOE 0.6).
- *Algenib IX*—Espandencia, a world of the Oikumene (BD 4).

ALKAID TWO a world where Graviton Corporation got in trouble for killing intelligent autochthons, violating the Doctrine of Responsibility (GAB). "Alkaid" is a traditional name for Eta Ursae Majoris, located 104 l.y. from Old Earth.

ALMACH star of planet Shaul in constellation Andromeda (FGB 5). The older name for Gamma Andromedae, found 350 l.y. from Old Earth.

ALMANATZ a planet of the Commonwealth (KT).

ALME world where Emphyrio was despot (E 17). Probably another name for Halma.

ALNITAK FIVE a colonized world (CHO). "Alnitak" is an old name for Zeta Orionis, located 1,300 l.y. from Old Earth.

ALODE a star visible from Halma (E 4).

ALOYSIUS a cosmopolitan world of the Oikumene (DP). Vega V; Lyra Sector; 25 l.y. from Old Earth.

DIAMETER: 7,340 miles.

SIDEREAL DAY: 19.836218 hours.

MASS: 0.86331 earths.

AXIAL TILT: 31.7° (producing Earth-like seasons with severe changes).

ATMOSPHERE: Dense and moist.

GEOGRAPHY: Nine continents, "Dorgan" the largest, "New Wexford" its chief city (PL 3). Or seven continents, the largest being "Marcy's Land" with chief city New Wexford, followed by Bodant's Land, Dimpey's Land, Llinliffet's Land (city Rath Eileann beside Lake Feamish), and the smallest is Gavin's Land with city Pontefract (F 1).

CITIES:

- Pontefract is the publishing/finance center of Vega system (BD 1), with Dunes spaceport nearby (BD 3).
- Rath Eileann details (F 2); Rath Eileann has a Darsh colony, "Wigaltown," nearby—the tavern "Tintle's Shade" gives visitors a hearty sample of Darsh culture and cuisine.

CURRENCY: SVU.

HISTORY: Among the first worlds to be colonized from Old Earth, initially by members of the Natural Universe Society. Then came a flurry of religious fanatics, most notably the Ambrosians, who founded the city Rath Eileann, and the Aloysian Order who arrived 40 years later (F 2) and renamed the planet after their patron saint. These two groups met and resolved their differences with the First Vegan War.

USEFUL TERMS:

Maasday—a day of the week.

Median—an hour name, like "noon," but it applies to an hour of evening, perhaps the first (BD 5).

St. Dulver's Day—a named day of the calendar.

Swister Day—a day of the week.

Throat-hole—apparently every Aloysian has one of these (KM 2).

ALPHANOR a cosmopolitan world of the Oikumene (DP). Rigel VIII; Orion Sector; 860 l.y. from Old Earth.

DIAMETER: 9,300 miles.

MASS: 1.02 earths.

MEAN DAY: 29 hours, 16 minutes, 29.4 seconds.

HYDROGRAPHY: 75%.

GEOGRAPHY: A large bright sea world with seven nearly contiguous continents (Phrygia, Umbria, Lusitania, Scythia, Etruria, Lydia, and Lycia) in a configuration suggesting the seven petals of a flower. But also Trans-Iskana, the south continent (BD 9).

Scythia, the largest and most sparsely populated continent, is considered the most bucolic by the folk of Umbria, Lusitania, and Lycia. Garreau Province (capital city Marquari) is the most isolated region of Scythia, fronting the Mystic Ocean and backed up into the Morgan Mountains. Marquari has bi-weekly airship flights to Taube, a sunny village on the shores of Jermin Bay (KM 3).

CITIES: The metropolis of Alphanor is Avente, with Sailmaker Beach to the north on Thaumaturge Ocean (BD 1).

GOVERNMENT: Pyramidal democracy. Alphanor is the capital planet of the Rigel Concourse (SK 4).

CURRENCY: SVU.

ALPHARD star, another name for Alpha Hydrae, 177 l.y. from Old Earth.

- *Alphard-Alpha*—a planet whose flora includes a type of flat sponge that absorbs rhenium (GAB).

- *Alphard*—alien homeworld where the sapients look like metal lobsters without claws or antennae (MMU).
- *Alphard VI*—the Oikumene planet Quantique, which see.
- *Alphard IX*—a Commonwealth world with seaweed processors (SJA).

ALPHECCA NINE an inhabited world of the Gaean Reach (ArS 1.1). "Alphecca" is a traditional name for Alpha Coronae Borealis, located 75 l.y. from Old Earth.

ALPHERATZ the earlier name for Alpha Andromedae, positioned 97 l.y. from Old Earth.
- *Alpheratz A*—a dry planet with oceans of the heavy gas neon kryptonite (FGB). It was settled by one of the Sons of Langtry, who gave rise to the Pherasic, also known as the Eagles, a race of highly mutated humans. (The other Langtry races are the Badau, the Koton, the Loristanese, and the Shaul.)
- *Alpheratz B*—a jungle world supplying the Eagles of Alpheratz A with agricultural products (FGB 5).
- *Alpheratz VI*—planet of the Oikumene, featuring the great Tri-Ocean Canal (FT 1).
- *Alpheratz IX*—a strange, non-Earth-like planet of the Commonwealth (TOB).

ALSCHAIN Beta Aquilae (MMU). Its fourteenth planet is Plais. "Alshain" (lacking the "C") is a real name for this star, which is located 45 l.y. from Old Earth.

ALTAIR humans from this star system recolonized Old Earth after a fallow period (LC). Located 17 l.y. from Old Earth.

ALVAN star mentioned during the rivalry between interstellar Blue and Kay (WB).

AMENARO solitary planet of Deneb Kaitos, considered by some to be the homeworld of mankind (E 19).

ANDROMEDA 469 an F6 star, also called "Martin Cordas" (MZ). It has two inhabited planets, Ethelrinda Cordas and Lucia Cordas.

ANDROMEDA 6011 IV a junction world of the Gaean Reach, located in Mircea's Wisp (ArS 6.1).

ANTAEUS a colonized world with vines 30 miles long (WLA).

ANTHONY PRINGLE'S WORLD an inhabited world of the Gaean Reach, located in the Argo Navis sector (EOE 8.3).

AQUILLA a region of the Gaean Reach, presumably named after the constellation seen from Old Earth (NL 10.4).

AQUILLA GB 1201 star of the Oikumene's near Beyond (KM 8). See SASANI.

AQUIN a blazing red star in the constellation Perseus Holding High the Head of Medusa (ArS 6.2). One of Medusa's eyes, the other being Cairre.

ARBELLO a world of the Gaean Reach (DTA 5).

ARBONETTA a world of the Gaean Reach where the people wear their hair in varnished ringlets (DTA 8).

ARCADY a planet of the Alastor Cluster famous for its carbuncle mines (W 2).

ARCHAEMANDRYX a highly metallic world inhabited by near-gaseous "ghosts" who live in colonies, each centered on a nucleus that eats uranium and emits nutritious radiation (KT).

ARCHIMBAL a Gaean Reach planet near Avente (Lu 11.2).
MAIN CITY: Organon.
SOCIETY: A population of communal groups, guided by comprehensive altruism. Taverns only serve non-alcoholic beverages, for example, barley water.
HISTORY: First visited by legendary locator Hans van der Veeke (Lu 11.3).

ARCTURUS star in Boötes Sector, 37 l.y. from Old Earth.

- *Arcturus IV*—an inhabited world of the Oikumene, it has the city Bugtown (BD 1).
- *Arcturus Five*—an inhabited world of the Cluster, an Earth-centered association (TB).

ARCTURUS LEGEND a world of the Gaean Reach (POC 6.0).

ARDEMIZIAN an inhabited world (ST 3).

ARGO NAVIS used as a sector of space, but historically this big constellation was broken into three smaller constellations: Carina, Puppis, and Vela.

ARGO NAVIS 14-AR-366 a yellow-white star, also known as Pharisse. Its sixth planet is Nion (EOE 8.2).

ARGO NAVIS 961 star commonly known in the Oikumene as "Cora" (F2). See DAR SAI, METHEL.

ARIES 44R951 alien inhabited system (MMU). The autochthons here look like big dry tumbleweeds, each with a hundred jellyfish tangled in it. They live on the surface of shallow lakes crusted over with algae. Males construct igloos of peat-moss on the shore.

ARIES SECTOR mention of the "middle reaches" of Aries in the Oikumene, with regard to Marhab (BD 1).

ARNEB Alpha Leporis (MMU). Alien inhabited system. The aliens here are globes of blue jelly, inside of which are seven balls of yellow light floating around three balls of red light. "Arneb" is a real name for this star, which is located 2,200 l.y. from Old Earth.

ASPERGILL an inhabited world of the Gaean Reach, located in Mircea's Wisp (ArS 9.1).

ASPIDISKE a real star also known as Iota Carinae, situated 690 l.y. from Old Earth.

- Aspidiske—planet of aliens (MMU).
- Aspidiske IV—a Gaean Reach transportation hub at the head of the Argo Navis sector (EOE 8.3).

ATREUS one of Sabria's two suns (GAB).

AUME an earlier name (or an alias) for the planet Halma (E 19).

AURIGA 225-G star, one of two candidates for Persigian (MMU).

AURIOL star of planet Pao (LP 1).

AVENTE a Gaean Reach planet near Mirsten (Lu 11.2).
MAIN CITY: Chancelade.
SOCIETY: A population of individualists.

AXELBARREN an inhabited planet of the Gaean Reach (NL 6.3).

AZUL a planet of the Commonwealth located in Sagittarius (TOB).

AZULIAS world of the Alastor Cluster (Ma 2).

B

BADAU an opulent blue-green planet orbiting Scheat, it possesses a thick atmosphere, high gravity, and it was originally claimed by one of the Sons of Langtry (FGB 1). The Badau are mutated humans, having short legs and hump-heads (FGB 2). They are one of the five Langtry races, the others being the Eagles, the Koton, the Loristanese, and the Shaul.

BAKAIMA one of the worlds allied against the Klau Empire in the Great Lenau-Lekthwan-Earth-Bakaima Coalition (GI 27).

BALIBEROS inhabited planet with a long history (GI 4).

BALLEN a bright star, orbited by Ballenkarch (ST 2).

BALLENKARCH settled by humans, an underdeveloped world with vast mineral wealth (ST 1).

BALMATH a planet of the Alastor Cluster, it is famous for its carved jade (Tr 17).

BANACRE a world of the Gaean Reach (DTA 3).

BAO world with autochthons (PF 6).

BARLEYCORN a world of the Rigel Concourse (SK 4).

BATEN KAITOS an alien inhabited system (MMU). "Baten Kaitos" is an old name for Zeta Ceti, located 260 l.y. from Old Earth.

BATMARSH an inhabited planet of the Polymark Cluster (LP 2).

BEAU AIRE a colonized planet (CHO).

BELAND an inhabited world near Kyril and Mangtse (ST 4). Beland humans are white-haired, loose-jointed, and have emerald-green eyes.

BELLA'S PRIDE a colonized world (AbS).

BELLATRIX V also known as Tranque (EOE 5.2). "Bellatrix" is an older name for Gamma Orionis, located 250 l.y. from Old Earth.

BELOTSI a world where sword-wielding humans fight club-bearing Brands, tall black humanoids with home-hives (NeP). The Brands are the warriors; at the hive, "genetrices" are twenty-foot monsters that crawl on hands and feet, having deadly jaws that snap; each hive has a Great Mother, slow moving but ferocious.

BERNAL a planet of the Oikumene famed for its flame-fighters, who wear varnished black plates with horns, cusps, and prongs in the manner of stag beetles (SK 9) and its elusive flame-maidens (KM 2). Their names seem to be military organizational: "Rank Olguin 92, File Mettier 6" and "Rank Sett 44, File Mettier 7" being two examples (KM 4).

BETHUNE PRESERVE a garden world of the Oikumene (DP). Corvus 892; Corvus Sector.

The only habitable world of fourteen planets around a yellow dwarf (BD 15), Bethune is a nature preserve with carefully controlled access. There are over 600 game and nature reserves, ranging from an entire continent to a single acre supporting the single and unique lillaw tree. Here is found Astrinch, a genus of humanoid autochthons with a wide variety of species, three examples being the 30-foot tall giants, the 8-foot tall types, and the small "puppet mandarins."

POPULATION: 5 million; Tanaquil city (BD 17).

FAUNA

- *Balt-ape*—ranging in size from ten to twenty feet tall, a vile-smelling white-skinned creature with splotches of black fur. Its head is half-bear, half-insect.
- *Lucifer*—nocturnal.
- *Printhene*—stalking carnivore.
- *Scalawag*—pack hunter, half-lizard, half-dog.
- *Scorposaur*—nocturnal.
- *Swamp-Walker*—purple and black creature with odd cloak of woven vegetation.
- *Three-armed swamp ape*
- *Triceratops Shanar* ("Shanar" is a Bethune continent).

CURRENCY: SVU.

BEYOND region outside the sphere of the Oikumene or the Gaean Reach. Worlds of the (Oikumene) Beyond include Bissom's End, Blue Planet, Brinktown, Caro, Grabhorne, Murchison, New Hope, Palo, Pharode, Providence, Sasani, Smade's Planet, Sogdian, Teehalt's Planet, Thamber, and Thumbnail Gulch. Stars include Carina LO-46, Ferrier's Cluster, and Sirneste Cluster.

Worlds of the (Gaean Reach) Beyond include Maske and Safronilla, and town Serafim.

BGD 1169 a distant star in Argo Navis IV (HL). Planet 2 has a paradox. Humans, who speak English, are living here in alien castle-like structures. Wild men in the forest are those who left the castles. Inside the castles, invisible servants tend to the humans. Secret History: ERJXKP XOB MBQP IFHB ELRPB ZXQP.

BHUTRA Gaean Reach star of planets Eiselbar, Dwet, and Zalmyre (MT 10).

BIG PLANET frontier world at time of Earth Central (BP, ShW). Probably in Virgo, as it is beyond Virginis Reef (BP 3). Innermost world of star Phaedra.

DIAMETER: 25,000 miles.

DENSITY: 2 g/cm³ (about the density of brick).

GRAVITY: Slightly over 1.

HYDROGRAPHY: 50%.

SATELLITES: None (ShW).

GOVERNMENT: Balkanized. At one point the Bajamum of Beaujolais seemed on the verge of unifying the planet; other contenders at that time included the Nomarch of Skene, the Gaypride Baron, and the Nine Wizards. Earth Enclave is the official spaceport and safest place.

TECHNOLOGY: Limited by lack of metal. While metal is very scarce on Big Planet, the system's three outer worlds are all extremely dense.

CURRENCY: Iron. A "groat" is a coin of .5 grams of iron, worth the value of a day's common toil (ShW 1).

HISTORY: Colonized at least 500 years before the story in *Big Planet*, and *Showboat World* takes place centuries later.

TRANSPORTATION: The monoline or "high-line" is an elevated ropeway along which cars with wind-sails and trolley-wheels run (BP 10). And the magnificent showboats of the lower Vissel River ("Cusp 23" in the planetary cartographical nomenclature) deserve mention as well.

Naisuka—what makes a person decide to do things for no reason whatsoever; the reason that is no reason at all.

Six-moon—a time period of about one month.

BISSOM'S END a dangerous world of the Beyond (DP). Carina LO-461 IV.

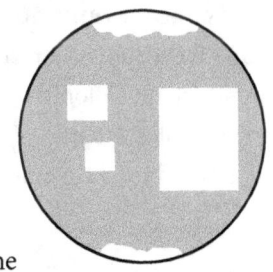

DIAMETER: Small (estimated 6,000 miles).

ATMOSPHERE: Earth-like.

GEOGRAPHY: A swampy world with a mountain chain circling the equator (KM 1).

POPULATION: Skouse, the principal town, has a population of around 3500.

HISTORY: Settled by Henry Bissom around the year 800, by the 1500s it had become the preserve of the Windle family, who lived in caves in the mountains behind Skouse. The world is notorious for "deweaseling" (killing IPCC agents).

BISTA one of the five moons around the colonized world of star Magda (WFM).

BLAISE a great blue star, also known as "the Blue-eyed Devil," orbited by Natrice (ArS 7.2).

BLANCHE a white star in Cancer, a double-star with Rouge, orbited by Noir and Jexjeka (TOB).

BLAZON a Whelm checkpoint for travelers to Numenes in Alastor Cluster (Ma 2).

BLENKINSOP, MOULDER 17 a world of the Gaean Reach, a junction for interstellar trade (POC 4.1). The star Moulder is orange, having 22 planets including the single habitable one.

GEOGRAPHY: Eight continents: polar, antipolar, four that are sodden marshes, and two with gentle terrain where the cities are located, each to the north of the hills, with the industrial yards still farther to the north (Lu 9.1).

POPULATION: Three thousand years after colonization, home to a dour, dark-visaged race: the Blenks. They live in five great cities and work at vast industrial yards that provide goods for half of the worlds in the local sector.

THREE CASTES
1. Shimerati, who live in palaces along the ridges of the southern highlands.
2. Hummers, high-level financiers and merchantilists, legal, medical, and technical professionals, and general intelligentsia. Their mansions are on the slopes of the highlands.
3. The working classes, who live in solid little bungalows arranged side by side in the cities.

There is little street traffic in the cities, where most Blenk ride the subway systems.

ART: Theater is king. In the city Cax is the vast theater Trevanian. Seating is by caste, with Shimerti in the high balcony, Hummers in the balcony, and the working classes on the floor.

BLUE-EYED DEVIL see BLAISE.

BLUE PLANET a world of the Beyond (SK 2).

BLUE-STAR homeworld of the alien Jangrill (MMU).

BLUE STAR ⚑ an interstellar nation locked in conflict with the Kay (WB). All names start with "B." Neutrals include Alvan, Canopus, Graemer, and Copenhag.

BLUE WORLD a lost world (BW).
HYDROGRAPHY: 100%. The shallows are 300+ feet deep. As a result, metal is virtually nonexistent. Colonists live on giant lily-pad plants called Floats.
SOCIETY: The Home Floats have a caste-based society.

The Blue World

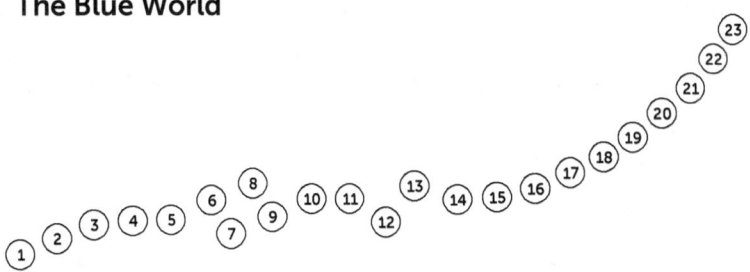

The Home Floats

1	Sciona	7	Wyebolt	13	The Bandings	19	Green Lamp
2	Almack	8	Lamp	14	Tranque	20	Fleurnoy
3	Parnassus	9	Sankston	15	Thrasneck	21	Aumerge
4	Populous Equity	10	Granolt	16	Bickle	22	Quincunx
5	Leumar	11	Apprise	17	Sumber	23	Fay
6	Maudelinda	12	Quatrefoil	18	Adelvine		

CASTES OF BLUE WORLD

High Castes	Intercessor (priests/sanitation, cleanliness), Hoodwink (semaphorists).
Middle Castes	Advertizerman (clan Belrod, deep divers), Anarchist, Bezzler (nobles?), Extorter, Felon (boat builders), Larcener (builders), Malpractor (dentist/doctors), Niggler (wood carvers), Procurer (emotional detachment), Scrivener (scholars), Swindler (fishermen).
Low Castes	Blackguard (sponge arbor builders), Hooligan (net makers), Incendiary (fiber and rope makers), Peculator (dye works), Smuggler (varnish makers).

GOVERNMENT: Each Float has direct democracy.

RELIGION: Sea-monster appeasement (King Kragen, the largest of the kragens).

TECHNOLOGY: Stone age without the stones, but the Floats communicate with each other by semaphore towers. Ingenious use of plant and animal materials, including human bones, to make tools and goods. Cultivation of food sponges.

HISTORY: Colonized twelve generations (175 years?) ago by a group of 200 prisoners from a cluster of twenty-five bright stars in the southern sky who were apparently bound for a prison world called "New Ossining." Somehow the prisoners overpowered the starship crew and crash landed their ship(s) into the waters of the Blue World. (See "Appendix XI: Linkages Between Texts.")

EXPORT: None.

CURRENCY: None (barter). Food sponges might come close to coinage.

BOGARDUS a planet of the Oikumene (F 14). "Bogardus" is another name for the star Theta Aurigae, so that is probably where it is located, 166 l.y. from Old Earth.

BONIFACE a cosmopolitan world of the Oikumene, former prison world of the Vegan system (DP). Vega VI; Lyra Sector; 25 l.y. from Old Earth.

Outermost and largest of the inhabited Vegan worlds, Boniface is gloomy and dank. In earlier times it was the dumping ground for atheists, incorrigibles, and irredeemables of Aloysius and Cuthbert. Port Swaven is the spaceport, and there are small towns Slayman, Cashel Creary, Nahutty, Kaw Doon, and Fiddletown (BD 8). Also World's Moil-Athmore Violet (BD 7).

AUTOCHTHONS: The Fojos, a new human species.

HISTORY: Administration of the penal colony was handled by the Order of St. Jedasias. The Fojos were inadvertently created by the "toughening" genetic experiments of one Abbot Nahut upon newly arrived convicts. By 1525 the Order of St. Jedasias is long extinct, but the Fojos still follow a variant of the Jedasian creed, and in every little Fojo village exists a square Jedasian church (BD 8).

USEFUL TERMS (FOJO SLANG)

Bosers—women.

Chut—fellow.

Coigel—penis.

Gautch—payment.

High Eye—heaven or God.

Prut—a long stocking cap.

Scarfer—a tough guy.

Slarsh—a pre-adolescent girl.

Slarsh-tit—a trifling amount.

Tiddling the deckers—doing house chores.
Twittle—the least bit.
Yetch—human.

BOSSOM'S WORLD a planet of the Gaean Reach (MT 9).

BRAN a giant orange star, its third world is Terce (POC 5.1).

BREAKNESS a cold, gray, mountainous planet orbiting a small white star in the Polymark Cluster (LP 6). Home to Breakness Institute, made up of several colleges, all ruled by a group of Dominies (or Wizards), competing with each other.

BRENGASTEL industrial world of the Klau (GI 20).

BRINKTOWN settlement on a criminal haven located in the North East Middle Beyond (SK 1). Perched on a volcanic butte overlooking a savage jungle of orange and black, the city was established by wanted criminals avoiding the Oikumene. Originally Brinktown was the last outpost, the jumping off point, but by 1404 it was just another world in the Middle Beyond.

LAW: In 1404, prisoners are merely locked out of the city. A single road leads from city to jungle. No prisoner ever ventures far from the gate. This institution seems to have vanished by 1524.

ART: Sumptious frontyard tombstones.

SOCIAL: Houses are multi-storied, most of them having three or four floors. Paper house-capes and paper slippers are worn inside of houses.

BRUSE-TANSEL: ALASTOR 1102 a world of the Alastor Cluster (Ma prologue). Population: 200,000, mostly in area of Lake Vain. Export: Dyeing fabric; four spaceports, the primary being at Carfaunge. Currency: Ozol.

BUGTOWN a city on Arcturus IV (BD 1).

C

CADWAL a Gaean Reach world (CAD). A planet of Syrene (yellow white star) of the Purple Rose System located mid-way along the Perseid Arm of the Galaxy.

TRIPLE STAR SYSTEM: Lorca (white dwarf), Sing (red giant), Syrene (three planets). Vaguely alluded to as being 100 l.y. from Old Earth (ArS 6.2), the actual distance is more likely to be 10,000+ l.y.

DIAMETER: 7,000 miles.

GRAVITY: Close to 1 g.

DENSITY (CALCULATED): 6.3 (High-Iron).

GEOGRAPHY: The three continents are Ecce (equatorial jungle), Deucas (northern temperate and largest), Throy (south polar to southern temperate). Araminta Station, an enclave of 100 square miles, is located on the east coast of Deucas; Stroma, a small Naturalist settlement, is located on Throy.

FAUNA: The banjee, an aggressive, tool-using, anthropomorphic creature, with language impervious to Gaean linguists.

POPULATION: Descendants of Naturalists are the citizens of Araminta and Stroma; menial labor provided by Yips, human descendants of offworld imported laborers who left the civilized enclaves to form illegal communities, the largest of which is the sprawling Yipton, a tourist attraction in its own right.

SOCIETY:

(Araminta) Upon reaching adult age those who fail to score high enough on the meritocratic grade will not become citizens and face emigration or a marginal existence at best. Cadwal is a nature preserve. The Life, Peace, and Freedom Party (or LPF) at Stroma is dedicated to the overthrow of the Cadwal Charter and opening continent Deucas to exploitation and settlement. They are called "Peefers."

(Yip) The Yips are a golden skinned, golden-haired, beautiful people who are indolent and lazy but will do anything if they are offered enough money.

GOVERNMENTS:

(Araminta) A meritocratic bureaucracy that has become corrupted by nepotism. There are six bureaus:

BUREAUS OF ARAMINTA

Bureau A	Records and statistics.
Bureau B	Patrols and surveys; police and security.
Bureau C	Taxonomy, cartography, natural science.
Bureau D	Domestic services.
Bureau E	Fiscal affairs (exports/imports).
Bureau F	Visitors' accommodations.

(Yip) A mysterious ruler known as the Oomphaw, a chieftain who has at his disposal an elite militia of Oomps, more formally known as the Oomphaw's Police Sergeantcy.

CURRENCY: Sol.

HISTORY: A nature preserve with limited tourism, colonized from Old Earth.

CRISIS: The existence of Yipton; plans for the mass deportation of Yips from Cadwell; the desire of bureaucrats to become aristocrats with vast plantations worked by Yips.

CAFFIN'S WORLD a Gaean Reach planet of Mircea's Wisp (ArS 7.1).

CAIRRE a blazing red star in the constellation of Perseus Holding High the Head of Medusa (ArS 6.2). Like Aquin, one of Medusa's eyes.

CALBYS a highly-ranked world raided by the Klau for Calbyssian slaves (GI 14). Non-Earth humans, the Calbyssians have purple-gold hair, and indeterminate sexes. They spend their free time trying to guess the sex of other Calbyssians while hiding their own.

CAMBERWELL one of twelve planets orbiting Robert Palmer's Star (brilliant white) located in the far edge of Cornu Sector of Ophiuchus (NL 1).

GEOGRAPHY: Four continents; Tanzig, the most important town.

POPULATION: Vongo gypsies—eighteen tribes roam the steppe and never bathe. They use music as magic against one another. There is even a separate caste of musician-assassins.

CURRENCY: Sol.

CAMBIASQ a world of the Gaean Reach (FT 1).

CAMBYSES a world of the Commonwealth where humans are sacrificed in religious practices (CG).

CANOPUS Alpha Carinae, brightest star in the southern constellations of Carina and Argo Navis. From Old Earth perhaps as close as 100 l.y., or as far as 300 l.y.

- *Canopus*—world of Blue Star era (WB).
- *Canopus III*—an inhabited world of the Oikumene (BD 13).
- *Canopus Four*—an inhabited planet dependant upon the Sons of Langtry for space-drives (FGB 2).
- *Canopus IX*—planet of the Gaean Reach (Th 3.2).
- *Canopus Planet*—world of the Gaean Reach (NL 6.3). Probably Canopus IX.

CAPELLA Alpha Aurigae, star in Auriga Sector, 42 l.y. from Old Earth.

- *Capella IV*—has the autochthon Bidrachate Dendicaps, furry, sulfur-eating bipeds (SO 1).
- *Capella V*—Maastricht (E 16).
- *Capella VI*—an inhabited world of the Oikumene, with the city Benitres (F 12).
- *Capella IX*—Tamar, a planet of the Gaean Reach.
- *Capella XII*—noteworthy for its great Equatorial Highway (HI 6).

CAPH "Caph" is an earlier name for Beta Cassiopeiae, 55 l.y. from Old Earth.

- *Caph III*—home of jeeks, creatures that eject a spurt of foul-smelling body tar as a defense (AC).
- *Caph IV*—a lively little world of the Oikumene (F 7).

CARINA 4269 star located in the constellation of Carina (CC 1). See TSCHAI.

CARINA LO-461 a greenish-yellow star in the Beyond (KM 1). See BISSOM'S END.

CARNEGIE TWELVE world with autochthons that look like armadillos (UM).

CARO a world of the Beyond (SK 10). It lies in a sector of space unclaimed by any of the Demon Princes. Mayor Janous Paragiglia of the city Desde pressed a crusade against the Demon Princes, prompting Malagate the Woe to make a sobering example of him.

CASSIOPEIA 993:9 a planet of the Gaean Reach (ArS 1.6). This is probably the ninth world of HD 993, a B8 star located in Cassiopeia, about 1,230 l.y. from Old Earth.

CASTLEGRAN an inhabited world near Beland and Cil (ST 11).

CEPHEUS 9621 a planet inhabited by the air-swimming Carboids (MMU).

CESTUS FQR910 yellow-orange sun of Rlaru (SO 12).

CETI 1620 an Oikumene sun commonly known as Fritz's Star (F 3).

CHAMANITA PLANET a world of the Gaean Reach where Yip labor is in demand (EOE 2.4).

CHANDARIA a world of the Commonwealth, it is an ancient planet with large oceans (SSS). It seems to be located about 3 l.y. from Fomalhaut, and as such it probably orbits CD -23° 1799, a class K7 V star that is 3.5 l.y. from Fomalhaut.

CHANKOZAR a world where human nations fight each other with cannon and galley (NeP). The nations of Belaclaw and Salomdek ally against Rac.

CHANNEL PLANET a world "full of ice and frost-fleas and the dullest aborigines in space" (POT). Administered by Earth System, it is bland and boring compared with Firsk.

CHASTAIN a cold planet where the alien Grays have fluid-gaseous helium bloodstreams (MMU).

CHROMOSPHORO Centauri 9518 (MMU). Alien inhabited system, where the autochthons have an upper half like a big red fish, surrounded by eighteen jointed legs, the knees at human eye level.

CHRYSANTHE a planet of the Rigel Concourse (SK 4).

CICELY an inhabited world of the Gaean Reach (DTA 5).

CIL a world inhabited by fairy-like humanoids (ST 5).

CIRGAMESÇ a small world of the Commonwealth, located 200 l.y. from Old Earth (SJA). (The name is not pronounced "Sirgamesk," so perhaps the proper pronunciation is more like "shir-JAW-mess," or even "Sir James.")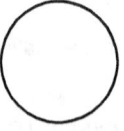

DIAMETER: It is not quite as big as Mars (which has a diameter of 4,200 miles).

ATMOSPHERE: None.

HISTORY: It was colonized by Javanese, Arab, and Malay settlers from Old Earth, who live in mountain valleys with lids over them. Thus the valley sultanates of Singhalût, Hadra, New Batavia, and Boeng-Bohôt; the Great Rift Colony of Sundaman.

TOURISM: There are ancient ruins from millions of years ago—when the atmosphere went, the population went with it.

USEFUL TERMS:

Adak—an obstacle to an irresistible emotion that leads to turbulence.

Amok—a person who, faced by an adak, resorts to killing.

Napaû—a philosophy where one finds meaning, life, and beauty in every aspect of the world.

Sjambak—a type of bandit/wizard who lives outside in the vacuum.

CIRSE green star of Marune, binary with Maddar (Ma 3).

CLANCTUS a planet of the Gaean Reach famous for its Glass Towns (ArS 1.6).

CLANTLALAN SYSTEM ⚑ in the period of the Tellurian Empire that pre-ceded the Commonwealth, the Clantlalans have a rival space empire (WT 1). Their home system has two stars, and is located out beyond Fomalhaut. The edge of their empire is a four-day flight away from Earth.

CLARENCE ATTIC a Gaean Reach world at the base of Mircea's Wisp in the constellation Pegasus (Th 3.3).

CLARENDON also known as Algenib IV, an inhabited planet of the Gaean Reach (EOE 0.6).

CLARI name, in Tschai universal, for the constellation in which Earth is lo-cated (SvW 2). If this is accurate, Clari is about the same as the constellation Cepheus (CC 3).

CLAVE II a Commonwealth world whose ULR messages to Polaris are routed through Dicantropus, as are messages from Polaris to Clave II (MD).

CLAVEROPS an alien homeworld (MMU). The autochthons are humanoid amphibians, sleek like seals, greenish-brown in color, with hands and feet like those of frogs.

CLEO 8 a high gravity world (HI 5).

CLUSTER ⚑ an Earth-centered stellar nation at time of contact with Haven (TB). Planets include Arcturus Five.

CLUSTER SI 1-715 a group of 29 stars seen from Sirene (MM).

CODIRON a colonized world of star Mintaka Sub-30 (AbS).
  ORBIT: Distant (sun is minute in sky).

MEAN DAY: 28 hours.

SEASONS: Likely none (due to distant orbit).

SATELLITES: One moon, small bright Sadiron.

CLIMATE: Windy and cold (CHO).

POPULATION: Delta is the largest city.

NOTES: "Mintaka" is an old name for Delta Orionis, a star 900 l.y. from Old Earth.

COLD EDGE a boundary of the Alastor Cluster, near the Fontinella Wisp (Ma 3).

COLUMBA a constellation containing Delora's World (EOE 3.3). Presumably the same Columba seen from Old Earth.

COMMONWEALTH 🏳 a galaxy-spanning nation extending outward over 2,000 l.y. from Old Earth. Its planets include Alpheratz IX, Azul, Cambyses, Chandaria, Clave II, Dicantropus, Duax, Eta Pisces, Exigencia, Fan, Formaferra, Gengillee, Gamma Scorpionis, Hard Luck Diggings, Hecate, Hither Sagittarius, Journey's End, Julian Wolters IV, Kokod, Kolama, Mallard 42, Moritaba, Naos, New Sudan, Omicron Ceti III, Padme, Pi Aquarii, Pi Sagittarius, Polaris, Rhodope, and Thaddeus XII. Presumably Gavnad, Hycithil, and Starlen are members as well. An important city is Starport, while the Hub is a resort hotel in deep space. Beyond the borders are Jexjeka, and Sclerotto Planet. See also TELLURIAN EMPIRE.

CURRENCY: Munit.

CONEXXA alien homeworld at Beta Trianguli (MMU). These aliens are close to human, but with copper skin, black lips and ears, and having glossy black fur on their shins. "Conexxa" is not a real star name, but Beta Trianguli is found 127 l.y. from Old Earth.

COPENHAG star or planet during the rivalry between interstellar Blue and Kay (WB).

COPUS a cosmopolitan world of the Oikumene (DP). Pi Cassiopeiae VIII; Cassiopeia Sector; 174 l.y. from Old Earth.

ETHNOGRAPHIC DETAIL: The Eginand of Copus are a human group whose women wear black metal sleeves on each finger joint (KM 8).

ARTS: Mersilin rugs from the Adar Mountains, Gypsy rugs from the Khajar Realm (BD 2).

CORA star, also known as Argo Navis 961 (F 2).
- *Cora II*—Dar Sai.
- *Cora III*—Methel.

CORALANGAN planet with the Olympic Mountains and the Songingk Desert (PF 6).

CORALASAN world with a red sea (WLA).

CORALYNE star of the reptilian Basics. See AERLITH.

CORDAS SYSTEM the star Martin Cordas and its inhabited worlds Lucia Cordas and Ethelrinda Cordas (MZ).

CORNU SECTOR region of Ophiuchus where Robert Palmer's Star is located (NL 1.1). This might refer to Taurus Poniatovii, an obsolete constellation next to Ophiuchus, since "cornu" is "the horn," used for "cornu ariets" (the horn of the ram Aries) and "cornu tauri" (the horn of the bull Taurus).

CORVUS 892 star, presumably located in the constellation Corvus (BD 15). A yellow dwarf, in a group of a dozen such stars, it has 14 planets including Bethune Preserve.

CROW Corvus, the constellation of Bethune Preserve (BD 14).

CUENOS NOTOS an Oikumene world where meat animals are raised (F 12).

CUTHBERT a cosmopolitan world of the Oikumene (DP). Vega IV; Lyra Sector; 25 l.y. from Old Earth. Humid and unpleasantly marshy, with few areas comfortably habitable, hence the sobriquet "Bug-Hunter's Paradise" (BD 8). City Conover (SK 3).

CYGNUS T342 star allegedly located in the Cygnus constellation (SK3). See EUVILLE.

CYTHEREA TEMPESTRE an inhabited world with large oceans and many islands, located in the Virgo sector (BD 3).

D

DADARNISSE JUNCTION a world of the Alastor Cluster, an intermediate stop between Marune and Bruse-Tansel (Ma 4).

DAMAR the moon of Halma, home to a species of intelligent humanoid aliens, the Damarans (E). Damar is a relatively inexpensive vacation resort. The Damar Puppets are living creations used as pets or performers, designed and bred by the Damarans.

DAMBROSILLA planet of the Gaean Reach, home to the notoriously prideful Overmen (NL 5.2).

DAR SAI a harsh world of the Oikumene (DP). Cora II; star Cora in Argo Navis.

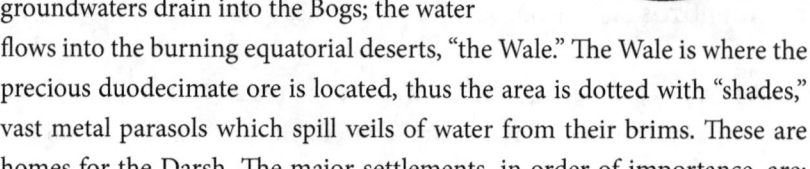

SATELLITES: One moon, named Mirassou.

GEOGRAPHY: Closer in orbit around Cora than Methel, Dar Sai has a more challenging setting. At the poles the winds howl in perpetual down-draft cyclones; the consequent groundwaters drain into the Bogs; the water flows into the burning equatorial deserts, "the Wale." The Wale is where the precious duodecimate ore is located, thus the area is dotted with "shades," vast metal parasols which spill veils of water from their brims. These are homes for the Darsh. The major settlements, in order of importance, are:

Serjuez, Wabber's Fountain, Dinkelstown, and Belfeser. Spaceport services are rudimentary.

SOCIETY: The Darsh are a gender polarized people. The women are strong and mustachioed and run their shades (titularly belonging to their husbands) like plantation manors. The men are miners of ore and are uniformly bald. Darsh marriage is an economic union lacking in sexual congress. Males and females have separate spheres—they don't even eat the same food or spend much time with members of the opposite sex. The moonlit desert is the amoratory playground where males seek young (pre-mustache) females and females seek young (pre-bald) males, while young ones seek young ones. Travelers beware—anyone found wandering in the desert at night will be assumed to be searching for sexual adventure.

GOVERNMENT: No central authority, although Methlen agencies maintain order in the major settlements. (See METHEL.)

LAW: The most vile crime is theft of a desert roller or a person's water supply. Murder and robbery are severely punished by exposure to desert fauna. Crimes of a sexual nature are not recognized as crimes.

ARTS: Darsh men have evolved a form of entertainment called "snavelry," a whip-dance involving a clownish whip-master and his troupe of naughty "bungle" boys. These acts are wildly popular among the men and disdained by the women.

SPORTS: Darsh men enjoy playing in and betting on "hadaul," a game of physical prowess and cunning played upon a prepared surface having three concentric circles and a pedestal. For more detail, see "Appendix II: Sports."

EXPORTS: Duodecimate ores (from the equatorial deserts) and offworld labor to Methel.

CURRENCY: SVU (and ores used locally for gambling).

USEFUL TERMS:

Ahagaree—an expensive Darsh spice from bog-algae.

Algaic Planks—construction material of made from compressed bog algae.

Asi achih—"And so it went," phrase used by Darsh men returning home at day's end.

Camboysse—a satyr of Darsh mythology.

Chelt—young Darsh girl.

Chichala—a rude term suggesting food prepared for and served to men.

Daffleday—a named day of the week.

Dirdolio—name of a calendar month.

Dumble—Darsh residence within a shade; clusters of domes.

Fust—body odor of Darsh men.

Goumbah—a man of vulgar futile stupidity (term used by Darsh women).

Iskish—term for a non-Darsh person.

Khoontz—an aged Darsh female; a virago.

Kitchet—post-adolescent, pre-mustache young Darsh woman.

Koruna—a fragrance applied by Darsh men to augment their fust.

Leino the Grandmother—a figure of Darsh mythology.

Meriander—a fragrance used by Darsh men to enhance their fust.

Mirmone—name of a calendar month.

Pittaugh the Sandsprite—an elemental of Darsh mythology.

Plambosh—the quality of pride; in Darsh men, a roguish swagger; in women, a studied inscrutability.

Rachepol—a "crop-ear," a person driven away from his native shade; an outcast.

Sansuun—the evening breeze.

Shrig—a bog animal larva that glows and dances; derogatory term for a dilettant.

Swagbottom—jocular, derogatory term for an old Darsh woman.

DARKLING REGIONS 🚩 an interstellar nation beyond both the Alastor Cluster and the Gaean Reach (Tr prolog).

DARYBANT an inhabited planet of the Gaean Reach (GPr 6).

DASHBOURNE PLANET a world of the Gaean Reach, far from Thesse (FT 4).

DAUNCY'S WORLD a Gaean Reach planet of Mircea's Wisp (ArS 1.5).

DAVID ALEXANDER'S PLANET an Oikumene world (F 1).

DELIA'S VALE a planet of the Gaean Reach (NL 13.2).

DELORA'S WORLD a Gaean Reach planet "at the back of Columba," famous for its sunsets (EOE 3.3).

DELTA AQUILA a star with an inhabited world in the time of the Tellurian Empire, it forms one end of the Delta Aquila-Sabik route (PBD). Properly Delta Aquilae, this star is 50 l.y. from Old Earth.

DELTA CORVI an alien inhabited system (MMU). The humanoid aliens here are tall and look rather crow-like with their black skin, but they lack beaks and have no feathers except for crests running down their necks. The star is found 87 l.y. from Old Earth.

DELTA RASALHAGUE a wealthy world of the Gaean Reach (DTA 2). Rasalhague, or "Ras Alhague" (meaning "Head of the Snake-Charmer") is another name for the star Alpha Ophiuchi. Since Rasalhague is not a constellation, then the "delta" probably does not refer to a star, and it might instead point to a fourth planet of Rasalhague. Rasalhague is 47 l.y. from Old Earth. (For what it is worth, Delta Ophiuchi is known as "Yed Prior," and is located 171 l.y. from Old Earth.)

DELTA TRIANGULI a star orbited by a couple of dead planets (FGB 8). It is 35 l.y. from Old Earth.

DENEB KAITOS star of planet Amenaro (E 19). Deneb Kaitos is another name for Beta Ceti, located 96 l.y. from Old Earth in the constellation of Cetus.

DENEB TEN a world colonized by humans after the invention of the Langtry space-drive (FGB 7). The resulting mutated humans are Labirites. Deneb is a name for Alpha Cygni, which lies 1,600 l.y. from Old Earth.

DENEBOLA star of Oikumene world Terranova (BD 3). Denebola is also known as Beta Leonis, and lies 36 l.y. from Old Earth.

DERARD a Gaean Reach world near Vermazen (POC 1.2).

DERDYRA an Oikumene planet (F 14).

DESERTA DELICTA a human-colonized desert planet (MMU).

DEULLE: ALASTOR 2121 a planet of the Alastor Cluster (Ma 2).

DIAMANTHA an unexciting inhabited planet of the Gaean Reach (GPr 2).

DIANDAS an orange star forming one eye of the constellation Gorcula the Dragonfish (BFM 6).

DIANTHE star of planet Vermazen (POC 2.1).

DICANTROPUS a desert world in a star system located between stars Clave and Polaris, with a lonely ULR message relay station serving the two (MD). It is also in a line between Alphard and Thuban.

CURRENCY: Munit.

Autochthons are owlish leather-gray little creatures, intelligent, capable of speech, that live in mounds.

DIMMICK a boring planet of the Gaean Reach (POC). Fifth world of Maudwell's Star, Leo JN-44.

A cloud-covered world so dull that the only interest to tourists is the weekly dogfights (POC 2.1). Despite the presence of several continents, the population is concentrated in a district surrounding the city Flajaret.

LAW: In earlier times, malefactors were dressed in boots, a breechclout, and a respirator before being discharged a metered distance out upon the algae mat that covers the ocean. The more flagrant the crime, the farther from shore was the culprit banished, to a maximum of five miles. The mat is home to a variety of noxious insects.

DIOGENES a world of the Rigel Concourse (SK 4).

DIOSOPHEDE a planet of the Gaean Reach, from which the Credential Renunciators fled to Mora, star of Maske and Skay (MT Preface).

DOUAUNE a small dead world circling Osmo (Ma 5). Another one is Haune.

DUAX a world of the Commonwealth (CG).

DUBHE an Oikumene planet relatively near Caph IV (F 7).

DUPTIS MAJOR a world of the Oikumene, known for its lime trees (BD 3).

DURDANE a planet of three dwarf stars: Sassetta (white), Ezeletta (red), and Zael (blue), just beyond Schiafarilla Cluster, coreward from Old Earth (DU).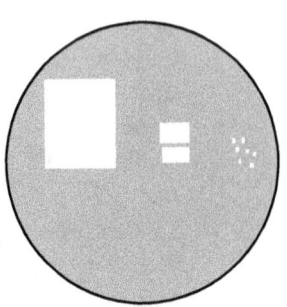

GEOGRAPHY: A low metal world (An 4) with four continents—Shant, Palasedra (south of Shant), Beljamar (a great archipelago east of Shant), and Caraz. Garwiy is a city of Shant famed for its purple glass towers.

POPULATION:

- *Colonists:* Human (in three regions).
- *Fringe Marauders:* Roguskhoi, strange humanoids of the wilderness. Their presence causes an international crisis between Shant and Palasedra.
- *Autochthons:* Ahulph.

GOVERNMENT: Balkanized. Shant and Palasedra are developed nations; Caraz is a sparsely settled continent, a frontier-land independent and unincorporated. Palasedra has a technological aristocracy, the Eagle-Dukes.

In Shant, sixty-two autonomous cantons are ruled over by the Anome, the Faceless Man, who has power of life and death over all citizens by way of their torcs (explosive-lined neck collars). A few of the cantons are listed below.

CANTONS OF SHANT, DURDANE

Canton	Notes
Amaze	Noted for musician competitions.
Bastern	The Chilites, a theocratic feudalism.
Burazhesq	Pacifistic sect Aglustids.
Cape	Old-age houses are notorious.
Conduce	
Dithihel	Ruled by women.

continued on following page

Durrume	
Faible	
Fenesq	
Fordume	Jade carvers.
Frill	Express themselves through flags.
Galwand	
Garwiy	Metropolis of Shant, first city of Durdane.
Gitanesq	
Glaiy	Primitive feudalism.
Glirris	Notorious for its vices.
Gorgash	
Haghead	
Haviosq	
Hinthe	
Ilway	
Lor-Asphen	
Maiy	Octagonal houses, with prestige shown by height of chimney.
Marestiy	
Maseach	Has city Maschein on south slope of the Hwan.
Morningshore	
Pagane	
Parthe	
Purple Fan	
Purple Stone	
Sable	
Seamus	Hot-tempered.
Shade	
Shalloran	
Shallou	A western canton.
Shker	Ruled by Diabolists.
Shkoriy	Mountainous.
Surrume	
Trestevan	
Wild Rose	

SOCIETY (SHANT): The freedom of anarchy tempered by the severity of autarchy. There is no central government beyond the Anome, who acts as an invisible judicial branch with a foundation of domestic surveillance.

LAW (SHANT): Each torc displays a personal color code sequence unique to each individual—this is the code which, transmitted by radio, will reach out and cause decapitation at the Anome's command. When people's heads are blown off they are assumed to have been investigated by the Anome, found guilty, and executed by remote control. The Anome has a secret number of deputies known as "Benevolences." The constabulary of Garwiy Aesthetic Corporation, known as the Discriminators, are the single sophisticated police force of Shant (BFM 1)—otherwise and in the main, each canton handles lesser crimes and punishments according to their own tastes.

ARTS (SHANT): "Ael'skian," the aesthetics of color, are highly developed in Shant.

SHANT COLOR SYMBOLOGY

Color(s)	Meaning
Blue, green, purple, gray	Optimism.
Browns	Unfavorable, tragic, elegant, or authoritative, depending on context.
Yellow	Color of death.
Red	Invisibility; red things are to be ignored.
White	Mystery, chastity, poverty, or anger, depending on circumstances.
Magenta	Grandeur.
Grayed pink	Omnipotence.
Brown and black	Emergency.
Caraz (a complex color of mottled black, maroon, and plum, with a silver-gray sheen)	Chaos, pain, and the macabre.

TRANSPORTATION (SHANT): Dirigible trains link the cantons together.

CURRENCY (SHANT): Florin.

SECRET HISTORY: Various Shant officials are JXKFMRIXQBA YV XPRQOX FKQBIFDBKQ XIFBK MXOXPFQBP COLJ XKLQEBO TLOIA. QEB HX XIFBKP, another group, XOB XQ TXO TFQE QEB XPRQOX; at one time long past QEB XPRQOX TBOB ALJFKXKQ, but QEB HX LSBOZXJB QEBJ XKA BKPIXSBA QEBJ. Now QEB XPRQOX RPB ERJXK ELPQP QL CFDEQ

XDXFKPQ QEB HX LK XKLQEBO TLOIA; QEB HX ZOBXQBA QEB OL-
DRPHELF QL FKCFIQOXQB AROAXKB and TFMB LRQ QEB PLROZB LC
ERJXKP RPBA YV QEB XPRQOX.

HISTORY OF DURDANE

Years Ago	Event
9,000	Colonists from Old Earth build the first Garwiy, initially dominated by Chama Reya.
	The Architectural Corporation dominates Garwiy.
4,000	Pure Boy religion founded.
	The Director Dynasties dominate Garwiy.
	The transitional Superdirectors dominate Garwiy.
	The Purple Kings dominate Garwiy, ending with the 4th Palasedran War.
2,100?	The Hundred Years War (over torcs).
2,000	The Anome founded after 6th Palasedran War.

USEFUL TERMS:

Aelsheur—air color.

Arusch'thain—a violet sunset with horizontal apple green clouds.

Chsein—conditioned recoil from a forbidden thought.

Druithine—a type of solitary wandering musician who never sings.

Feovhre—a violet sunset calm and cloudless.

Gorusjurhe—a flaring, flamboyant sunset encompassing the whole sky.

Heizhen—a sunset heavily overcast except for a ribbon of clarity at the west, through which the sun sets.

Kial'este—a color mingling violet and blue, signifying snobbishness.

Shergorszhe—like "gorusjurhe" but with cumulus clouds in the east.

Sunuschein—reckless, feckless gaity, tinged with fatalism and tragic despair.

Zuweshekar—to use a musical instrument with such passion that the music takes on a life of its own.

DAYS OF THE WEEK

Durdane	English
Ettaday	Saturday?
Shristday	Sunday?
Kyalisday	
Zaelday	

DUSA a hard little Gean Reach world located at the brink of Beyond (Lu 3.4).

DWET a Gaean Reach planet, being a swampy world of Bhutra (MT 11).

DYS a moonless world of the Gaean Reach (DTA 5).

E

EARTH see OLD EARTH.

EARTH CENTRAL 🏴 government of Earth in era of *Big Planet* (BP 1). Other planets include Index.

EARTH SYSTEM 🏴 government in era of "Potters of Firsk." Other worlds include Channel Planet.

EIFAL an inhabited world, where ice-skating is practiced (GI 4).

EISELBAR a tourist world of the Gaean Reach (MT 10). The planets Dwet and Zalmyre, next out in orbit, are also very developed tourist locations. Bhutra star; Constellation Quincunx.

SOCIETY: All people wear adjuncts that play musical themes selected by the wearer. Standard themes include Stately Mien; Joviality; Pensive Dreams; Skylark Song; Receptiveness to Novel Ideas; Proud Assertion; Caprice and Original Whimsy; Quest for Love; Verve and Vivacity; Condolences; The Glory of Beauty; and others. There is a toggle for quarter of the day (morning, afternoon, evening, and night) and another for degree of companionship (solitude, boon companions, erotic proximities, and crowds). One's personal music is called "chotz."

ARTS: Sensitivity to "chords" of monochromatic light.

FAUNA: The famous slimes of Eiselbar are gaudy in color and rumored to be lethal to humans. Luckily they stay on the sand, so tourists won't be troubled if they only remain on the raised glass walkways.

Husler—honorific applied to both men and women. Eiselbar lacks castes, status being a direct function of wealth.

Katch—the masculine Eisel headgear, a rimless hat of pleated cloth.

ELFLAND a planet of the Rigel Concourse (SK 4).

ELLENT: ALASTOR 485 a world of the Alastor Cluster, home to the human Boles (Tr 5). The great majority of Boles are left-handed. Most Boles are devoutly religious and their place of perdition is the Black Ocean at the South Pole of Ellent, where submarine creatures house the souls of the damned. On Ellent, to eat wet food is to encompass within oneself a clutch of vile influences. No Bole eats fish.

EMERAUD a colonized planet (CHO).

ENDYMION'S LUTE a constellation seen from Cadwal (ArS 1.6). Old Sol is located at its center.

ENGSTEN an inhabited planet of the Terrestrial Empire (AC).

EPSILON SAGITTAE star of the Oikumene planet Verlaren (F 3). It is in Sagitta sector, 473 l.y. from Old Earth.

ERDIC SECTOR ⚑ a stellar nation beyond both the Alastor Cluster and the Gaean Reach (Tr prolog).

ERGARD a Gaean Reach planet notable for its high population density (POC epilogue).

ERIDANUS 2932 Haven's sun (TB).

ERIDANUS BG12-IV planet, also known as Skylark prison world (SO 9). The star might be 12 G. Eridani, an F2 V star located 154 l.y. from Old Earth.

ESPANDENCIA Algenib IX, a world of the Oikumene (BD 4).

ETA PISCES a star of the Commonwealth (SPA). Properly Eta Piscium, located 150 l.y. from Old Earth.

ETA SCORPIONIS a star with a planet of feuding tribesmen, so the Iszic breed watchtower trees especially for them (HI 5). This is probably a reference to Eta Scorpii, located 74 l.y. from Old Earth.

ETAMIN NINE original homeworld of the Meks, laborers for the Castles of Old Earth (LC 1.3). "Etamin" is one of the traditional names for Gamma Draconis, located 154 l.y. from Old Earth.

ETHELRINDA CORDAS sixth planet of Andromeda 469, an F6 star called Martin Cordas (MZ).

SATELLITES: Three moons: one a pale blue, the second large and apple yellow, the third a fat golden sequin.

GEOGRAPHY: A single vast continent, two large islands, a spatter of smaller islands. The western island is Agostino Cordas, the eastern one is Juanita Cordas. The big continent is Robal Cordas, mostly wilderness, but the west coast has Corda Federation (five cities).

EUVILLE a world of the Oikumene (DP). Cygnus T342; Cygnus Sector.

An unpleasant and psychotic population dwells here in five cities: Oni, Me, Che, Dun, and Ve; each built in pentagonal form radiating outward from a central five-sided citadel. The spaceport, located on a remote island, is named "Orifice" (SK 3). No passports are used—to visit a city, one must have a colored star tattooed on his or her forehead. "To visit all five cities the prospective tourist must display five stars: orange, black, mauve, yellow and green."

CURRENCY: SVU.

EXAR an inhabited planet (CM 1).

EXIGENCIA an Earth-like planet of the Commonwealth (TOB).

EZELETTA red dwarf star of Durdane (An 2).

F

FADER a hidden world of the Gaean Reach (NL). Night Lamp III.

SATELLITES: Two moons.

GEOGRAPHY: Single continent in southern hemisphere; the only spaceport, Flad, separated from the only city, Romarth, by a vast wasteland populated by dangerous nomads.

POPULATION:

- *Decadent Colonists:* Roums (human aristocrats), each born into one of forty-two Houses or Septs, including Urd, Ephrim, Ramy, Stam, Slayard, Sadaj, Carraw, Soumarjian (extinct), Immir, Methune (extinct), and Torres (extinct).
- *Managers:* Grichkin, sports of Seishanee (ratio of 200:1).
- *Laborers:* Seishanee (bio-engineered). Asexual, docile.
- *Nomad Barbarians:* Loklor (failed attempt at bio-engineered servants). Seven feet tall.
- *Encroaching Invaders:* White "house-ghouls" (another bio-engineering mistake).

EXPORTS: Minerals (mined by Seishanee) primarily, but the life books could be worth considerably more (see History below).

CURRENCY: Not used, but sols have some value.

HISTORY: Fader was colonized 5,000 years ago in a remote location by people bent on isolation and privacy. The Roum set themselves up as an aristocracy with an army of bio-engineered servants, the Seishanee, to labor for them. After 2,000 years they developed a fashion of each person writing a "life book," hand-written and lavishly illustrated, to be shelved in the ancestral mansion after the author's death. This tradition lasted for a thousand years or more, ending only with the Bad Times, a century of sly murder and gruesome dungeons that finished the High Era of Roum Civilization. Currently many mansions are abandoned, home to the subterranean white "house ghouls." The Roum occasionally have pitched battles against the ghouls but seem unable to exterminate them.

HISTORY OF FADER	
Year	*Event*
25,000	Fader colonized.
27,000	High Era begins.
27,500	Taubry of Methune writes his life book.
28,000	The Bad Times.

CRISIS: Decline and decadence seem terminal. Two possible avenues of recovery are FKZOBXPBA QOXAB (TFQE CXABO OBZBFSFKD JXOHBQ SXIRB CLO FQP BUMLOQP) and LMBKFKD QEB MIXKBQ QL QLROFPJ.

FAJANE a world famous for its ammoniacal storms (E 2).

FALLORNE a planet located at the far side of the Gaean Reach from Maz (DTA 8).

FAN an Earth-like world of the Commonwealth (TOB), it is often called "the Pleasure Planet" (WT 3). Mylitta is its chief city and starport (SAN).

FANUCHE a world of the Gaean Reach (DTA 8).

FARO a star of Glory (DSB).

FAYENCE STREAM a region of the Gaean Reach (DTA 3).

FEI a low gravity world (HI 5).

FELL planet three of Ramus, a giant red star (CM). Geographically, there is a North Polar Desert, and the jungle-surrounded continent Kalhua, with the chief city Huamalpai on the western rim. In rural Kalhua there is a human group, the Oros, who are said to be insane. Flora: seed pods that are great globes, bubbles, behaving like helium balloons (CM 8).

FENIM a blazing star in Miraldra the Enchantress, a constellation seen from Koryphon (GPr 3).

FENN inhabited marshy world, port city Momart (SU). The gravity here is .6 g.

FERRIER'S CLUSTER a star cluster of the Beyond (SK 10). It was the center of the sector allotted to the Demon Prince Malagate the Woe, a sector that includes planets Grabhorne and Providence.

FIAME a planet of the Rigel Concourse (SK 4).

FIAMETTA a planet of the Gaean Reach, it circles Kaneel Verd, the so-called "Green Star" (POC 7.1).

SATELLITES: Three moons.

GEOGRAPHY: Port Sweetfleur is 1,000 miles south of Port Girandole. One hundred miles east of Girandole, a region of rocky crags and high meadows called the Moabite Cloudlands. A declining population of Chan Overmen still live there in old manor houses, but many manors are abandoned, their gardens still guarded by ghost chaser statues of jade. The Chan Overmen appear to have a hypnotic gaze that can stun their victims (POC 7.4).

ART: The ghost chaser statues XOB XZQRXIIV IFSFKD ZOBXQROBP MBQOFCFBA FKQL QLOMFA ILKDBSFQV.

FIAMIFER common name of one of the structural features of the Alastor Cluster (W 2). Zeck is located here.

FIDESKE a small dead star, companion to Cora, which disintegrated and seeded Methel and Dar Sai with duodecimates, and created the moon Shanitra (F 7).

FIIR a world ruled by Priest-kings (NeP).

FIRE PLANET a world of the Polymark Cluster inhabited by the Dinghals, who are are reportedly cowards (LP 16).

FIRSK a low-tech planet administered by Earth System (POT).
> SIZE: Medium.
> GRAVITY: Near 1 g.
> METALS: Scarce.
> GEOGRAPHY: A single equatorial continent shaped like a dumbbell. The main city Penolpan is located a few miles in from the South Sea and is laced with canals of green water.
> AUTOCHTHONS: The Mi-Tuun, amber-skinned humanoids; the Potters, pale, red-haired humanoids of the hills.
> ART: The Potters live in the hills, using volcanic heat to bake their wares. They also incorporate the bones of the deceased into their clay, and they will resort to kidnapping and murder if the flow of natural deaths proves too few. "The soul lives forever in the pot it beautifies."

FIVE WORLDS the planets of the different Sons of Langtry (FGB 1): Alpheratz A, Badau, Koton, Loristan, and Shaul. Or a group of famously mysterious planets seldom seen by humanity, also known as the Five Jeng Worlds (E 2; 4).

FLESSELRIG a Gaean Reach world that is an important commercial and financial center of its sector, located near Nilo-May (NL 13.10).

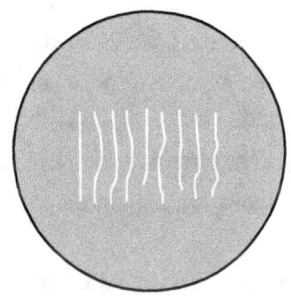

FLUTER a planet of the Gaean Reach, it circles the golden star Frametta (POC epilogue).
> SIDEREAL DAY: 28 hours (Lu 2.2).
> GEOGRAPHY: Fluter has nine narrow continents running north to south in one hemisphere, the other half of the planet being covered with ocean (Lu 3.1).
> POPULATION: Flauts live in back-country villages (POC epilogue). Corocoro, the spaceport town, is inhabited by a hybrid race mixed of Flauts and offworlders. They regard themselves as highly sophisticated aristocrats, with wealth derived from the tourist trade. The world population is limited to 99,000.

SETTLEMENTS: One hundred and forty-seven villages scattered at random across the nine continents, along with a special node surrounding the Coro-coro spaceport on Continent Five (Lu 3.2). Coro-coro is an oversized village. The best hotel in Coro-coro is the O-Shar-Shan, but it has no running hot water. Arrivals at the spaceport are allowed visitor's permits of 30 days' duration (Lu 2.2).

LAW: "Civil Agents" police Coro-coro; "Land Agents" watch over campers and excursionists (Lu 3.2).

THE THREE ORDERS OF PUNISHMENT	
The first order	Public chastisement.
The second order	Disgrace, confiscation of all property, expulsion from Fluter dressed only in a bramble.
The third order	Death by subaqueation in Sharler's Pond.

HISTORY: The Terrible Times was a period when murder was used to bring the population down to the target level (Lu 4.1).

FOMALHAUT star, Alpha Piscis Austrini, found 25 l.y. from Old Earth.
- *Fomalhaut IV*—Rhodope, a planet of the Commonwealth (SSS).
- *Sandusk*—a world of the Oikumene.

FORMAFERRA a strange, non-Earth-like planet of the Commonwealth (TOB).

FRAMETTA the star of Fluter (POC epilogue).

FRANTOCK a Gaean Reach planet, where archaeological shards are gathered at the Palisades (Lu 12.4).

FRITZ'S STAR also known in the Oikumene as Ceti 1620 (F 3). Its fifth planet, Hyaspis, is inhabited.

FRUMS an inhabited planet where slaves taken from Ballenkarch are used as bodyguards (ST 4).

FURAD a star of Marune in the Alastor Cluster (Ma 3).

G

GAEAN REACH ⚑ an interstellar nation on the Orion Arm reaching out in a 5,000+ l.y. radius from Old Earth, with territories on the Perseus arm (e.g., Cadwal). Bounded by the Great Hole/Zangwill Reef toward the Galactic East and three nations at other points: Alastor Cluster (toward the Galactic Rim); Liss, and Olefract (precise locations unknown, but probably toward either the Galactic Core or Galactic West).

CURRENCY: Gaean currency is the SVU (Standard Value Unit), the SLU (Standard Labor Unit: the value of an hour of unskilled labor under standard conditions), and the Sol, all being roughly equal in value (US $8 to $10, circa A.D. 2000). The 10-SVU banknote is purple, the 50 is orange. The units of small change include the three-piece (worth three-quarters of an SVU) and finally the zink (or "centim"), the worth of a man's labor for one Gaean minute.

TIME: While a Gaean hour equals an Earth hour, it seems that a Gaean hour is divided into 100 Gaean minutes (each being thus around 36 Earth seconds). The Gaean minute itself is divided into 100 Gaean seconds (making each a fleeting .36 Earth seconds).

CALENDAR OF GAEAN STANDARD TIME	
Gaean	*English*
Ianiario	January
Ferario	February
March	March
Mariel	April
May	May
Iulian	June
July	July
	August
	September
	October
	November
	December

Name	Metal	Metal for Our Days
(Ain) Ort	Iron	Tuesday
(Ain) Tzein	Zinc	n.a. *
(Ain) Ing	Lead	Saturday
(Ain) Glimmet	Tin	Thursday
(Ain) Verd	Copper	Friday
(Ain) Milden	Silver	Monday
(Ain) Smollen	Gold	Sunday

* Quicksilver is the metal for Wednesday.

PLANETS OF THE GAEAN REACH: Alcide, Alcydon, Algenib IV, Alphecca Nine, Andromeda 6011 IV, Anthony Pringle's World, Arbello, Arbonetta, Archimbal, Arcturus Legend, Aspergill, Aspidiske IV, Avente, Axelbarren, Banacre, Bellatrix V, Blenkinsop, Bossom's World, Cadwal, Caffin's World, Camberwell, Cambiasq, Canopus IX, Canopus Planet, Capella IX, Cassiopeia 993:9, Chamanita Planet, Cicely, Clanctus, Clarence Attic, Clarendon, Dambrosilla, Darybant, Dashbourne Planet, Dauncy's World, Delia's Vale, Delora's World, Delta Rasalhague, Derard, Diamantha, Dimmick, Diosophede, Dusa, Dwet, Dys, Eiselbar, Ergard, Fader, Fallorne, Fanuche, Fiametta, Flesselrig, Fluter, Frantock, Gallingale, Gaude Phodelilus IV, Gietersmond, Glamfyre, John Preston's World, Kars, Kodaira, Komard, Koryphon, Kyril (POC), Ladaque-Royal, Lakhme Verde, Lavendry, Liliander's Home, Lusbarren, Lutus, Madlock, Mariah, Marmonfyre, Mauberley, Maz, McDoodle's Planet, Merakin, Mildred's Blue World, Mirsten, Montroy, Morbihan, Morlock, Mossambey, Moulder 17, Moulton's World, Murtsey, Naharius, Natrice, New Calvary, Neroli, Nilo-May, Nion, Numoy, Old Earth, Old Kharay, Old Lumas, Olfane, Orvil, Paghorn, Perseus TT-652-IV, Pharisse VI, Pharistane, Phasis, Phrist, Plaise, Pranilla, Protagne, Rhea, Rosalia, Safronilla, Sagittarius FFC 32-DE-2930, Saint Wilmin, Sansevere, Sarbane, Scropus, Skalkemond, Soum, Spangard, Star Home, Sussea, Sylvanus, Tamar, Tanquil, Tassadero, Taubry, Terce, Terence Dowling's World, Tex Wyndham's Planet, Thesse, Tran, Tranque, Trasnoy, Tyrhoon, Ushant, Varsilla, Vermazen, Virgo AXX-1 Thirteen, Welters, Wicker, Wittenmond, Xanarre, Xanthenoros, Yaphet, and Zalmyre.

USEFUL TERMS:

Domine—a common term of address for persons of distinguished or exalted station (abbreviated Dm.).

Ton-ton eskoy—"the grotesque sometimes reaches such exalted levels that it becomes almost sublime" (Lu 8.2).

Visfer—a common term of address (abbreviated Vv.).

GALLINGALE a planet of the Gaean Reach (NL).

SATELLITE: Moon "Mish."

GEOGRAPHY: Thanet, primary city of Gallingale.

SOCIETY: Obsessively focused upon "striving" for "comporture"—the personal quest to increase status via social clubs or "ledges." People wear lapel pins and badges showing their club affiliations. Those who refuse to participate in striving are labeled "nimps" and generally command no respect.

GALLINGALE LEDGE HIERARCHY

The Sempiternals (high aristocracy)	Tattermen, Clam Muffins, and Quantors (this club is limited to nine members).
Aristocracy	Bon-tons, Palindrome, Girandoles, and Lemurians.
Lower aristocracy	Bustamone, Val Verde, Sasselton Tigers, Sick Chickens, and Scythians.
Lowest respectables	"Four Quadrants of the Squared Circle" —the Kahulibahs, the Zonkers, the Bad Gang, and the Naturals.
Middle status	Underwoods and Jinkers.
Middle status	Human Ingrates, Safardips, and Black Hats.
Middle status	Parnassians and Spalpeens.
Modest status	Persimmons, Zouaves, and Golliwogs.
Lowest rung	Junior Service League.
Outsiders	nimps

(Note: Altroverts are an odd case, not shown here.)

CURRENCY: Sol.

GAMMA ERIDANI star of the Oikumene planet Reis, it lies 150 l.y. from Old Earth (F 3).

GAMMA GRUS an alien inhabited system, where the Grus Gammans have five sexes (MMU). Properly Gamma Gruis, 230 l.y. from Old Earth.

GAMMA SCORPIONIS a Commonwealth star with more than one habitable planet (TOB). Properly "Gamma Scorpii," which is the original Bayer designation for what is now known as Sigma Librae, located 290 l.y. from Old Earth.

GANGALAYA an inhabited world (E 17).

GARUUN one of 19 moons of Nion (EOE 9.2).

GAUDE PHODELILUS IV an inhabited planet of the Gaean Reach (ArS 4.7). Home of the Laddakees.

GAVNAD the sixth planet of Delta Aquilae in the Tellurian Empire period prior to the Commonwealth (PBD). The star is 50 l.y. from Old Earth.

GEIDEON one of Sabria's two suns, along with Atreus (GAB).

GENGILLEE a strange, non-Earth-like planet of the Commonwealth (TOB).

GHER a psionic entity that is at war with the nopals (NOP). From Earth its star system, a red sun with a single world, is located in the direction of Perseus. It turns out that the gher controls the Tauptu group of the Xaxans.

GHH'LEKTHWA a world of golden-skinned humanoids who live in places floating in the sky and are strict vegetarians (GOG). Earth humans pronounce it Lekthwa, which see.

GHNARUMEN an independent alien world of the Oikumene (DP). Lambda Gruis III; Grus Sector; 242 l.y. from Old Earth.
    An Earth-like world, off-limits to humans. It is the home of the Star Kings, who "evolved from amphibious lizards who lived in wet holes" (SK 10), but in a rather plant-like fashion, "the young develop as pods in the

armpits" (SK 8). As one of the species known to have attained faster-than-light stardrive earlier than humanity, the Star Kings might be responsible for Monument Cliff on Xi Puppis X or Mystery Grotto on Earth's Moon (KM 3).

HISTORY OF GHNARUMEN	
Years Ago	*Event*
100,000	Proto-Star Kings visit Earth and take some Neanderthals back to Ghnarumen, where evolutionary pressures change both species.
50,000	Star Kings deliver to Earth some of their altered humans, which we call "Cro-Magnon" (SK 8).

GIANSAR an inhabited world (ST 9). "Giansar" is a real name for the last star in the tail of Draco, Lambda Draconis, 114 l.y. from Old Earth.

GIANT'S SCIMITAR a constellation seen from Halma (E 4).

GIETERSMOND a world of the Gaean Reach, being one of three Sister Planets of Jinkens Star. The people who live here are called Giets and they special-ize in technics (FT 6; 9). Fauna include antler fish, corkscrew ticks, and Flamboyard, a species of ostrich-like bipeds that eat fruit.

GILBERT'S GREEN STAR a Gaean Reach sun in Perseus with an unusual green tint thought to be created by heavy metal ions in the stellar atmosphere (Th 3.2). It has 11 planets, with Yaphet the only one habitable by humans.

GLAMFYRE a world near the edge of the Gaean Reach, to galactic north of Jack Chandler's Gulf (DTA 2).

GLANTZEN FIVE a world beyond the Skiaffarilla Cluster from Durdane (As 2).

GLORY a planet with chaotic daylight (DSB). Glory is Earth-like except for being in a system with four suns: Red Robundus, Urban (yellow-green), Maude (white dwarf), and Faro. The movements of the suns makes for a highly irregular pattern of light and darkness.

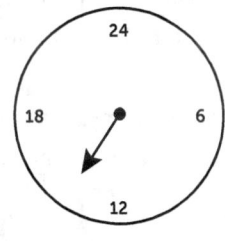

Originally settled 500 years ago by humans who became the Flits, goat-herds on the Grand Montagne. A more recent arrival is the Gospel Colony, who have brought civilization in the form of houses and canals, and standard time in the form of The Clock on Salvation Bluff. There are 72,000 colonists in Glory City, which boasts the Glory City space-port as well as a rest home. The Flits have Fleetville, the ruinous remains of their original settlement, and New Town, a tidy area built by the colonists for Flit use.

GODAG homeworld of the Blue Chasch (CC 8).

GOMEISA Beta Canis Minor, properly Beta Canis Minoris (MMU). The aliens of this system are ten-foot pontoons, each with an iron sail. They live in an ocean of mercury and are charged electrically. Gomeisa is a real name for this star, which is found 162 l.y. from Old Earth.

GONDWANA alien homeworld where the autochthons are monosexual (MMU).

GOODBY PLACE a structural feature of the Alastor Cluster (W 2).

GORCULA THE DRAGONFISH a constellation seen from Durdane, its "eyes" are the stars Alasen and Diandes (BFM 6).

GORGON'S TUSK a structural feature and/or route of the Alastor Cluster, it includes the planets Wyst, Hilp, and Lambeter (W 12).

GOSHEN a planet of the Rigel Concourse (SK 4).

GRABHORNE a world of the Beyond where the Demon Prince Attel Malagate maintained a plantation worked by slaves (SK 10). This was an area of space claimed by Malagate, and Providence was another planet found there.

GRAEMER SYSTEM an inhabited star system during the rivalry between interstellar Blue and Kay (WB).

GRAY WORLD: ALASTOR 1740 a world once ruled by Mad King Zag, who was ultimately subdued by the Whelm (Tr 3).

GREAT DARK CLOUD an area of interstellar space between Lekthwa and Old Earth (GI 2).

GREAT EEL a twisting constellation visible from Araminta Station (ArS 4.5).

GREAT HOLE a vast emptiness in the eastern fringe of the Gaean Reach (MT Preface). See STAR MAP COLLECTION.

GREAT LONESOME GULF a vast region of vacant space separating Pegasus from the Perseid Arm and Mircea's Wisp (Th 7.1). Also known as Shimwald Gulf.

GREEN-RASSINS a planet where the human race has mutated far from Earth's norms (FGB 4).

GREEN STAR a world of the Oikumene (BD 9); a world or star in Alastor Cluster (Tr 7); common name for sun Kaneel Verd in the Gaean Reach (POC 7.1).

GRGLASH Eta Cassiopeiae (MMU). Alien inhabited system. The aliens appear more human than they are: their basic chemistry is siliconic; their skulls are furnaces, flames shoot out of holes in their scalps, looking like beautiful orange hair. "Grglash" is not a real name, whereas Eta Cassiopeiae is also known by the real name "Achird."

GRIFFEIDES a magnificent constellation seen from Koryphon (GPr 3).

GROPUS a Commonwealth world known for its mountains (SJA).

GYRGUS a constellation seen from Koryphon (GPr 8).

H

HALLOWMEDE a world where mercenary troops may be hired (LP 9).

HALMA a planet of a star located beyond the Mirabilis Cluster from Old Earth (E). Morgan is another planet in the system.

SATELLITES: One moon, Damar, home to an alien race of puppet makers.

GEOGRAPHY: North Continent, South Continent, and the Mang Islands. North Continent has at least three nations: Fortinone, Bayron (east of Fortinone), and Bauredel (north of Fortinone). The capital of Fortinone is Ambroy, precincts of which still have ruins from ancient wars.

POPULATION (FORTINONE):

- *Colonists:* 3,000,000 "recipients" (human).
- *Invaders:* 200 lords, 400 ladies and lordlings (humanoid).
- *Autochthons:* The elusive wirwan (humanoid).

GOVERNMENT: Overlord (alien) welfare state, each lord with a utility fief—Spay (communications), Chaluz (energy), Flowan (water), Overtrend (transit), Underline (sewerage), and Boimarc (trade).

LAW: (Fortinone) A vagrant is expelled into Bayron. A smuggler is expelled into the Alkali Flats. The worst criminals are expelled into Bauredel (technically, the first two inches of Bauredel).

SOCIETY: The alien lords keep to their eyries, skeletal towers over ancient ruins, or are guarded by their gargoyle-like Garrion (known Damar creations) when moving among commoners. Day to day affairs are handled by the welfare agency, the numerous guilds, and the Finukan temple. Noncuperative or "noncup" is the term for "a nonrecipient of welfare benefits, reputedly all Chaoticists, anarchists, thieves, swindlers, whoremongers" (E 3).

RELIGION: The Finukan temple requires leaps and bounds of a strenuously physical variety ("halma" is Greek: to leap, spring). There is the mysterious Glyph and the enigmatic Finuka (E 7). But there is also the legend of Emphyrio, a man who dared to face the alien overlords and was killed for

The City of Ambroy

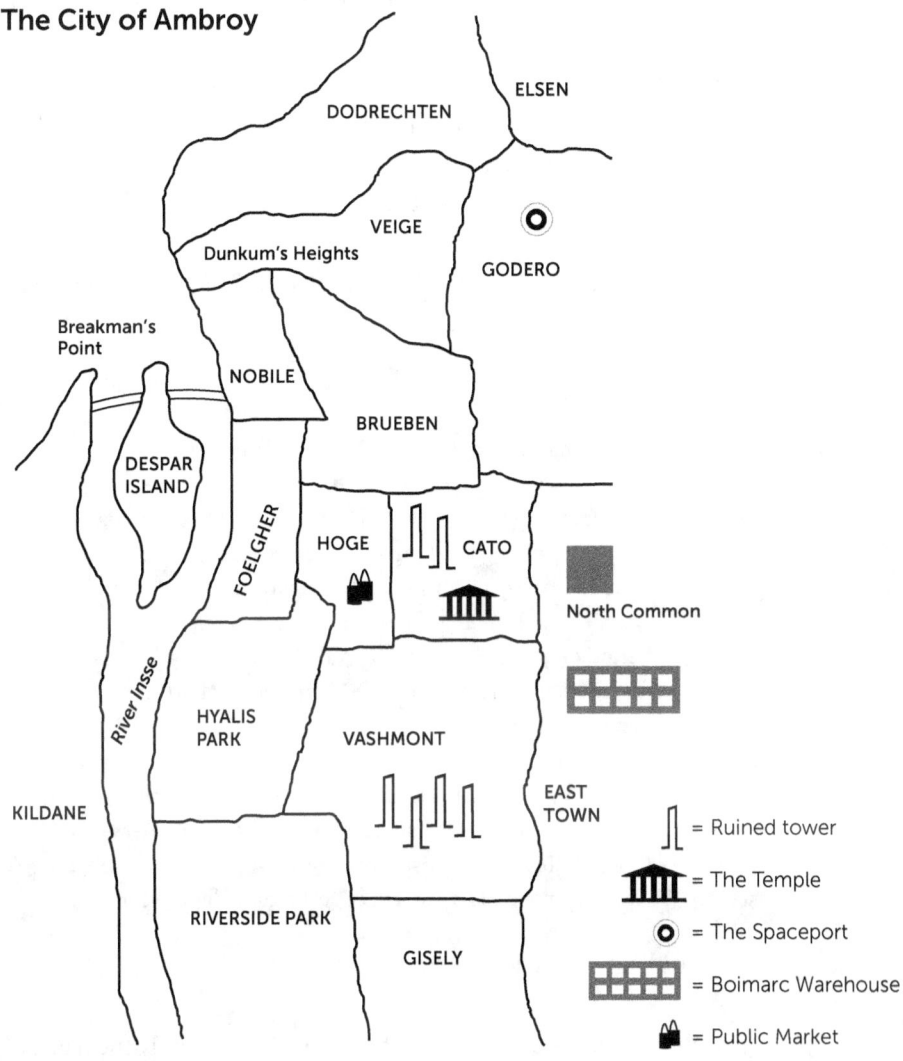

ELSEN

DODRECHTEN

VEIGE

Dunkum's Heights

GODERO

Breakman's Point

NOBILE

BRUEBEN

DESPAR ISLAND

FOELGHER

HOGE

CATO

North Common

River Insse

HYALIS PARK

VASHMONT

EAST TOWN

KILDANE

RIVERSIDE PARK

GISELY

⌐∟ = Ruined tower

🏛 = The Temple

◉ = The Spaceport

▦ = Boimarc Warehouse

🏪 = Public Market

speaking of peace—yet after his death the peace infected the overlords and the tyrants became like men.

ARTS: Puppet shows are very popular and utilize synthetic creatures manufactured by the autochthons of Damar.

TECHNOLOGY: While the lords have access to interstellar technology, for the common people all work is purposefully kept as labor intensive as possible (so as to prevent loss of jobs due to innovation).

EXPORTS: Highest quality handmade art objects, ultimately purchased by offworld museums (for example, one on Maastricht, Capella V), which then declare them priceless and license mass produced copies which are sold for a price slightly under that which the original artisan received for his labor.

CURRENCY: Vouchers, used on Halma only, sequins (E 5), and interplanetary exchange units called valuta (E 16).

TAX: 1.18 per cent.

TERMS OF ADDRESS: "Recipient," abbreviated "Rt" (E 3) for commoners, "Redemptionist" or "Lord" for aristocrats.

HISTORY OF HALMA

Years Ago	Event
5,000	Damarans have colonies on Halma (E 20).
4,000	Damarans expelled by star wanderers (E 20).
3,500	Damaran supersoldiers (Wirwan) come to retake Halma but star wanderers have gone, humans are there (E 20).
2,000	"Emphyrio" legend written, referring to Halma as "Aume" or "Home" and Damar as "Sigil" (E 19).
??	Period of Wars. The Dreadful War. The Star Wars. Fortinone vs. Bauredel. Fortinone vs. the Mang Islands. Fortinone vs. Lankenburg (E 5).
1,500	The Empire Wars. The last war, with Emperor Riskanie and the White-eyed Men, results in the destruction of the city Ambroy. Then the lords arrive in spaceships and set all in order (E 5).
1,300	Clarence Tovanesko (historical figure) lived (E 5).
1,250	Anti-duping laws go into effect, forbidding duplication.

SECRET HISTORY: The lords XOB AXJXOFXK ZOBXQFLKP.

HAN probably the name of the planet of the Han, it is certainly the name of the people and their god (TEM). See MAGARA TARATEMPOS.

HARD LUCK DIGGINGS possible name for a mining planet of the Commonwealth, a place with a slow-heaving, milk-white ocean (HLD). Flights to this outpost come straight from Starport. There are two settlements, Diggings A and Diggings B. Fauna include panther-like creatures, as well as four-armed apes, and rodents.

HARDACRES a planet of the Rigel Concourse (SK 4).

HAUNE a small dead world orbiting Osmo (Ma 5). Another one is Douaune.

HAVEN a shipwreck colony on the single planet of Eridanus 2932 (TB).
An Earth-like world, it was colonized during the Era of Great Excursives, when over-under space drives had first come into use. Haven was founded by the 63 survivors of the *Etruria* having gotten lost on the way to Rigel. After 271 years the population is 300 million. Their holy books are The Ten Books, a simple encyclopedia of Earth. At the time of recontact there were 7,000 years of history on Earth, and no wars to speak of since the Hieratic League broke up (sometime in the previous 271 years).

HECATE a world of the Commonwealth with some unusual authochthons called Meths (CG).

HEPHAESTOS a planet in the Commonwealth, or near it (TOB).

HERIARTES a star visible from Halma (E 4).

HILP a world of the Alastor Cluster, next from Wyst on a route called the Gorgon's Tusk (W 12).

HIMAT an inhabited planet (E 4).

HISTHORBO THE SNAKE a constellation seen from Durdane (As 6). The world Kahei is located therein.

HITHER SAGITTARIUS a region of empty space in the Commonwealth (CG).

HOME PLANETS ⚑ an interstellar nation that seems to be a precursor to the Oikumene (MM). Polypolis, a city of Old Earth, seems to be its capital. The currency is the UMI. (See "Appendix XI: Linkages Between Texts.")

HOME WORLDS the planets that produced the criminals who settled the Blue World (BW 10); the planets in the Gaean Reach that supplied the original settlers of the Alastor Cluster (W 5); also the human-populated planets orbiting Altair from which the Castle-builders came to Old Earth (LC 2).

HSI a red star involved in the rapid departure of the Fesa from Tschai, perhaps by going nova (Pn 12).

HUB a deep-space resort hotel floating in the Commonwealth's Hither Sagittarius, the Hub looks like a model of a very complex molecule, a cluster of bubbles in a web of metal (CG).

HYASPIS a world of the Oikumene, being the fifth planet of Fritz's Star also known as Ceti 1620 (F 3).

HYCITHIL a world of the Tellurian Empire phase, and presumably the Commonwealth that followed it (WT 3). It is famous for its Magic Groves.

HYDRA GRA 4442 star of planet Yan (SO 11). This might be a typo for G44 in Hydra, a K3 III (giant) star 419 l.y. from Old Earth, or it might be a typo for G42 in Hydra, a K2 III (giant) star 352 l.y. from Old Earth.

| I

IDORA an Oikumene planet, being the eleventh world of Sadal Suud (KM 6).

ILLUCANTE a planet of the Alastor Cluster (Tr 4).

IMAGE an inhabited world of the Rigel Concourse (SK 4).

IMBER a world of the Alastor Cluster (Ma 2).

INDEX a world on the way from Old Earth to Big Planet (BP 3).

INTERCHANGE the establishment at Sasani where ransoms are paid for kidnap victims (DP). There are six grades of suites at the prison/hotel:

GRADES OF SUITES

Grade	Notes
AA	The "Imperial Gardens."
A	
B	Allows full use of the establishment's recreational activities as well as a modicum of privacy.
C	
D	
E	For those who await a slaver's offer.

The cuisine is of "eight standard categories," including "classic," the cuisine of "Alphanor, West Earth, and perhaps a third of the population of the Oikumene" (KM 8).

"Guests" have a fifteen-day period of prime redemption, after which they are declared "available" and may be purchased by independent entrepreneurs. After a certain period, unless board and room bills are regularly met, the management may be forced to release custody to an independent entrepreneur for the extent of those bills.

PRICES OF GUESTS

Guest	Price
A nine year old boy and a seven year old girl, siblings.	20,000 to 30,000 SVU for the pair.
An heir.	40,000 SVU.
A young woman, handsome.	9,000 SVU (a rare bargain).

INTERSTELLAR NATIONS Alastor Cluster, Blue Star, Clantlalan, Cluster, Commonwealth, Darkling Regions, Earth Central, Earth System, Erdic Sector, Gaean Reach, Home Planets, Kay (of Kay System), Klau Empire, Lekthwa, Liss, Oikumene, Olefract, Phalid, Primarchic, Rubrimar Cluster, System, Tellurian Empire, and Terrestrial Empire.

IRTA a world of the Oikumene, being a planet of frozen salt tundra (BD 3).

ISTA one of the five moons around the colonized world of star Magda (WFM).

ISZM third planet (HI 10) of Xi Aurigae (HI 5). House trees are grown here. House breeding began 200,000 years ago (HI 4). The Iszic are descendants of tree-pod dwelling amphibians, and have segmented eyes. Useful term: Sainh, an honorific suffix added to a name.

IXAX Earth-like planet of the Xaxans, amphibious humanoids involved in a long war against the nopals, psionic entities (NOP). The fighting is between two groups of Xaxans: the Tauptu (or "purged ones") and the Chitumih (those possessed by nopals). After 100 years of warfare, the Tauptu achieve local victory but their world is in ruins. The Tauptu must rid Nopalgarth of nopals.

J

JACK CHANDLER'S GULF a region of the Gaean Reach (DTA 2).

JAMIVETTA a bleak world where moss is farmed on the tundra (ST 1).

JENA an inhabited planet (CM). The Clas of Jena are humans of Hyarnimmic ancestry, as are the Overmen of Maxus.

JEOL an inhabited world (GI 5).

JEXJEKA an airless planet located outside the Commonwealth in "Cancer 3/2" (TOB). It is the sole planet of a system with three stars: Rouge (a red giant), Blanche (a white star), and Noir (Blanche's dark companion). Jexjeka's year is 82 days, and it circles Rouge so that for half of the year, two suns shine during the day, and for the other half, Rouge shines by day and Blanche shines by "night."

JEZEBEL a planet of the Rigel Concourse (SK 4).

JHERIPUR Omega Crucis (MMU). Alien inhabited system. Autochthons here are humanoid, four feet tall, three feet wide, yellow as butter, completely hairless. ("Jheripur" is not a real star name, nor is "Omega Crucis.")

JINGKENS STAR a very large yellow star located for the Gaean Reach by Gieter Jingkens during the Great Expansion (FT 6). It has several dozen planets, three of them the so-called Sister Planets (Wittenmond, Gietersmond, and Skalkamond), each alike in size, mass, density, atmosphere, climate, and land-water ratios. Other worlds include Wicker and Lutus.

TERMS: "Merner," the usual polite appellative of the Jingkens' worlds (FT 11).

JINGLES "the Jingles" is a region in the Argo Navis sector (EOE 8.3).

JOHN PRESTON'S WORLD an inhabited planet of the Gaean Reach (ArS 1.4).

JONAPAH a star with a number of quiet little planets where the blossoms are soft pastel pink, green, blue, and yellow (ST 8).

JOURNAL a world of the Polymark Cluster that serves as a transportation hub (LP 9).

JOURNEY'S END a world of the Commonwealth (CG).

JUDITH IV a planet of the Commonwealth (KT).

JUGURTHA a world of rehabilitation farms, far away from Old Earth (AC).

JULIAN WOLTERS IV a strange, non-Earth-like planet of the Commonwealth (TOB).

JUNCTION a deep space station equidistant from Kyril, Mangtse, and Ballenkarch (ST 4).
Located on the Mangste-Thombul-Beland and Frum-Outer System traffic lanes, it is a very convenient way station or transfer point. A polyhedron one mile in diameter, it is famous for the Nineteen Gardens. The Celestium offers food and music of many local worlds. More shady attractions include Perfume Park (a brothel catering to women), the rather dangerous Tier Three (a bordello catering to men), and the very dangerous Arena (ST 7).

K

KAHEI homeworld of the alien Ka (As 9). The insectoidal parasites the asutra invaded Kahei and enslaved the Ka. Over time the Ka reversed the roles, and the asutra expelled from Kahei went to Durdane. The Ka created QEB ERJXKLFA OLDRPHELF and sent them to AROAXKB to destroy QEB ERJXK race (As 11).

KANDASPE a planet of Alastor Cluster located in the realm of Corë of the Four Bosoms near Zeck (W 10).

KANEEL VERD also known as Green Star of the Gaean Reach, orbited by Fiametta (POC 7.1).

KARNFRAY an inhabited planet of the Kay System (WB).

KARS a planet of the Gaean Reach, Perseus TT-652-IV (Th 6.6).

KAUS AUSTRALIS an alien inhabited system (MMU). This is a star's real name, but it is given as being "Eta Sagitarii," when it is more properly Epsilon Sagitarii, located 143 l.y. from Old Earth.

KAVANAF an inhabited planet of the Kay System (WB).

KAY SYSTEM the home system of the Kay, an interstellar group in rivalry with Blue Star (WB). All names start with "K." The star is called Kay, and it has nine worlds, six of them inhabited.
1. *Kool*—too hot for life.
2. *Kavanaf?*
3. *Koblenz?*
4. *Karnfray?*
5. *Kerrykirk*—capital world.
6. *Kelmet*—a world with domed cities.
7. *Kith*—a planet with domed cities.

8. *Kinsle*—an ammonia giant.
9. *Konbald*—an ammonia giant.

KELCE an inhabited world with vegetation colored black, gray, and white (ST 8).

KELMET a world of domed cities in the Kay System (WB).

KERRYKIRK the capital world of the Kay System (WB).

KILLARNEY Vega system penal satellite (KM 2).

KINSLE a gas giant of the Kay System (WB).

KITH a planet of domed cities in the Kay System (WB).

KLAU EMPIRE ⚑ an interstellar slaver state of 42 worlds (GI). Klau Planet is one week's travel from Magarak (GI 12). The Klau have four subspecies: Big Klau, Little Klau, Bornghalese, and Podruods. Podruods are the troops, the guards, the fighters.

KOBLENZ an inhabited planet of the Kay System (WB).

KODAIRA a Gaean Reach alias for the planet Naharius (POC 1.2).

KOETHENA a highly ranked world raided by Klau slavers, home to human-oids (GI 14).

KOKOD a planet of the Commonwealth (KW). Located at Pi Sagittarii, it is a small world with Earth-like gravity, featuring two-foot tall humanoid au-tochthons organized into hive-like "tumbles." Their technology is stone-age but their rules of warfare are elaborate and ritualized.

KOLAMA a Commonwealth planet that is a wilderness being made into a resort (SPA). Located at Eta Pisces [sic], it sports flying dragons and other dangerous monsters.

KOMARD a planet of the Gaean Reach (POC 4.1).

KOMRED Oikumene star, also known as Epsilon Sagittae (F3). See VERLAREN.

KONBALD a gas giant world of the Kay System (WB).

KOOL a planet in the Kay System, ironically too hot for life (WB).

KOON'S HOLE a large-scale feature of the Alastor Cluster (W 2).

KORDECKER 343 star system between Phalid and Earth, said to be in Sagittarius (PF 1).

KORYPHON a world of the Gaean Reach, far from the Alastor Cluster (GPr 8).

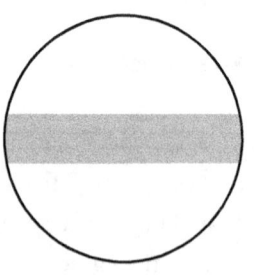

    STAR: Methuen.

    GEOGRAPHY: There are two continents, Uaia to the north and Szintarre to the south. On Uaia, the Uldras inhabit the Alouan, a wide band along the southern littoral. To their north the nomadic Wind-runners sail their two- and three-masted wagons across the Palga plateau. South of Uaia, across the Persimmon Sea, lies Sziatarre. It boasts the capital city Olanje, home to both the cosmopolitan Outkers as well as the government, the Mull.

    GOVERNMENT: The Mull, a council of thirteen nobles, rules (in theory) all of Koryphon from Olanje.

    POPULATION:

- *Aristocracy:* the Eng'sharatz ("the revered masters of large domains" or simply "land barons") of the Alouan Domains (descended from space pirates).
- *Offworlders:* Outakers (human offworlders in the cosmopolitan city Olanje at equator).
- *Displaced colonists:* Uldras (humans who live on the margins of the Alouan Domains). Their skin is gray (the men dye theirs an ultramarine blue) and their hair is orange.

- *Nomads:* Wind-runners (humans who sail windcarts across the northern plains and practice wind magic). They domesticate and offer for sale erjins that are especially massive and docile.
- *Autochthons:* Erjins, who use telepathy with each other (humans break them before using them as slaves) and morphotes (weird violent creatures that aficionados like to watch in the wild).

CURRENCY: SVU.

HISTORY: Two hundred years ago space pirates forced the Submission Treaties upon the Uldras and took choice land that became the Alouan Domains. The recent Pan-Uldra uprising is fostered by political party the Retent Uldras (also known as Blues), led by the mysterious Gray Prince.

SECRET HISTORY: Morphotes XOB QORB XRQLZEQELKP, erjins XOB QEB PMXZB MFOXQBP TEL ZLKNRBOBA QEBJ XDBP XDL—YLQE EXSB ABDBKBOXQBA LSBO QEB JFIIBKKFX.

USEFUL TERMS:

Ahariszeio—a divinity of the Wind-runners of the Palga.

Aurau—untranslatable; said of a tribesman afflicted with revulsion against civilized restrictions, and sometimes of a caged animal yearning for freedom.

Dreuwhy—untranslatable ancient Welsh; a self-induced mood of morose extra-human intensity in which any grotesque excess of conduct is possible.

Karoo—Uldra festivities, lasting a day and a night or three days/nights in the case of a Grand Karoo.

Sarai—untranslatable; a limitless expanse of land or water which makes one want to travel.

Xheng—untranslatable; a dark emotion of "horror-lust" or sadism.

KOTO an oyster-white planet orbiting Mirach, it was settled by Sons of Langtry (FGB 2). The Koton are a race of mutated humans with saucer-like eyes, one of the Langtry races. They are famed for their cruelty. (The other Langtry races are the Badau, the Eagles, the Loristanese, and the Shaul.)

KROKINOLE a cosmopolitan world of the
Oikumene (DP). Rigel XIV; Orion Sector; 860 l.y.
from Old Earth.

DIAMETER: 9,450 miles.

MASS: 1.23 earths.

MEAN DAY: 22 hours, 16 minutes, 48.9
seconds.

YEAR: 1,642 Earth-years (KM 8).

Third largest planet of the Concourse, and sometimes considered
the most beautiful. Krokinole might well be the most diverse, both geographically and ethnically. (Krokinole [KROA-kih-noal] is the name of a
Canadian boardgame that is like tiddly winks.)

GEOGRAPHY: Two large continents (Borkland and Sankland); six smaller
continents (Cumberland, Layland, Gardena, Mergenthaler, Hopland, and
Skakerland).

NATURAL MARVELS: Crystal Pinnacles of Bize Parish, the Card River
Falls of Dinker Parish (both in Cumberland); the Hole through the World
(North State, Sankland); the Undersea Forest (off the coast of Iksemand,
Skakerland); and Mount Jovah (in the Highlands of Gardena), the tallest
mountain of the Concourse (42,102 feet above sea level). The presence of
this last makes Krokinole a likely candidate for the world originally named
"Lord Bulwer-Lytton" by Sir Julian: "Most impressive perhaps are the New
Gramian Mountains on the North Continent of Lord Bulwer-Lytton" (SK 4).

POPULATION:

- *Human:* Skakerland was first settled by a schismatic cult of the
  Skakers who went to Olliphane. The remarkable Imps settled the
  Highlands of Gardena. Cumberland is the region of the talented
  and industrious Whitelocks. The Druid Banquers wander the
  tundras of North Hopland. Other groups include the Arcadians,
  Batthalese, Singhels, Oporto Fishermen, Jansenists, and Ancient
  Alans, to name just a few.
- *Autochthons:* The near-extinct Super-beasts, with their unique
  semaphore communicatory system, their boats, baskets,
  ornamental knots, and committee organization (KM 5).

CURRENCY: SVU.

KYRIL the homeworld of the Druids, where the Tree of Life grows (ST). About 1,000 l.y. from Old Earth, toward the galactic rim, beyond the Unicorn Gulf.

POPULATION: Ethnically they correspond to the ancient Caucasian race of the Mediterranean branch.

GOVERNMENT: Religious dictatorship.

SOCIETY:

- *Druids*—two million priests.
- *The Laity*—five billion peasants.

FLORA: The Tree of Life is something of a galactic wonder. With a trunk five miles in diameter, it stretches twelve miles into the sky.

TECHNOLOGY: Primitive. Imported aircars used by the druids are kept in barely working repair.

CURRENCY: Stiple (planetary only).

KYRIL a Gaean Reach planet of star Rhys (Lu 11.5).

SATELLITES: Three dim moons (Lu 11.4).

Holy Mountain is a dying volcano, a place where pilgrims from across the Gaean Reach walk a five-year course and earn themselves the honorific title "rondler" (POC 4.2).

L

LADAQUE-ROYAL a planet of the Gaean Reach, Sagittarius FFC 32-DE-2930 (NL 11.2).

LAKHME VERDE a Gaean Reach world where each village supports at least one orchestra (NL 9.3).

LAMBDA GRUS properly Lambda Gruis, a star located 242 l.y. from Old Earth (SK 1). See GHNARUMEN.

LAMBETER a world in the Gorgon's Tusk of the Alastor Cluster (W 12). Starships leaving Balad on Wyst invariably go to Hilp and then to Lambeter.

LAOOME'S WORLD out beyond Fomalhaut, past the fringe of the Clantlalan System, a yellow star with a single desert planet (WT). Possessing breathable air and standard gravity, it is home to only Laoome, an ancient alien exiled from his homeworld Narfilhet.

LAVENDRY a Gaean Reach planet in a system near Fluter (Lu 9.7). Main city: Ocean City.

LEKTHWA 🚩 a highly ranked planet of non-Earth humanoids who are technologically advanced and highly civilized (GI 1). Known as Ghh'lekthwa by the Lekthwans, who have gold skin and silver hair.

One Earth year equals 2.6 years on Lekthwa, meaning that the planet orbits its star in 140 days, which suggests a much closer orbit, comparable to a point between Mercury and Venus. Its sun is Skyl.

Their interstellar nation, a contemporary of the Klau Empire, has three worlds.

Their language is shaped by "characterizations," a play of eyes, eyebrows, and eyelashes. There are nearly 100 characterizations, 62 of them termed "basic" and the rest are called "optionals." Basics include "Sedate Counsel" and "Statistician," while among the optionals can be found "Smiling Sunrise," "Playful Kitten," and "The Solitary One."

HISTORY: Several hundred thousand years ago, Lekthwa had a period called "The Era of Insanity" when the white-haired people of the south and the golden-haired people of the north warred against each other (GG). Subsequently the two peoples became well mingled.

LENAU a planet of non-Earth humanoids raided by the Klau (GI 2). The Lenape are small, fat, yellow-brown humanoids used as technician slaves on Magarak (GI 19).

LENNOX IV a Commonwealth planet where the Yellow-Bounding tree grows (TOB).

LEO 4A563 star, one of two possibilities for Persigian (MMU).

LEO JN-44 Maudwell's Star, in the Gaean Reach (POC 2.1).

LIAD slowest of the five moons (furthest in orbit) in Magda system (WFM).

LILIANDER'S HOME inhabited planet of Mircea's Wisp in the Gaean Reach (ArS 6.1).

LILIMEL one of Nion's 19 moons.

LISS ⚑ an alien interstellar nation, contemporary to the Gaean Reach (DTA). The Liss are xenophobic to the point of obsession. See also OLEFRACT.

LOJUK a planet of Fitzsimmon's Star where the Tellurian Space Navy has a base (PF 2). Located near Canopus. (Gliese 253, a class G7 V star, is 10 l.y. from Canopus.)

LORCA white dwarf star, binary with Sing, in the Purple Rose System (ArS 1.0).

LORGAN a world of the Oikumene, featuring Boomaraw College and the Neuster Ocean (KM 8).

LORISTAN planet of Adhil, it is a small, mountainous world settled by one of the Sons of Langtry (FGB 2). The Loristanese are a race of butter-colored mutated humans, one of the five Langtry races (the others being the Badau, the Eagles, the Koton, and the Shaul). Interstellar merchants, they are rumored to be telepathic.

LUCIA CORDAS an inhabited world, seventh planet of Andromeda 469 (MZ).

LUPUS 23 II an Oikumene world, second planet of Lupus 23, in the Lupus Sector (PL 4). The autochthons produce beautiful "supplication slabs."

LUSBARREN a world of the Gaean Reach where fishing is a major industry (DTA 3).

LUTUS a planet of the Gaean Reach (FT 9).

LYONNESSE highly industrialized world of the Rigel Concourse, famous for its monumental Gnome Iron Works (SK 3; 5).

M

MAASTRICHT Capella V (E 4). This world has a monopoly on artworks from Halma. "The Fourteen" are the most wealthy and important merchants. Fauna include air-snakes.

MADAGASCAR a world of the Rigel Concourse (SK 4).

MADDAR star of Marune, binary with Circe in Alastor Cluster (Ma 3).

MADLOCK a Gaean Reach planet (Lu 9.2).

MADURA world where the Battle of the Birds took place (E 2).

MAEVE a planet settled by humans (FGB 6).

MAGARAK a Klau planet of slave-driven mining and manufacturing (GI 2). There are slaves here from planets Perdu, Calbys, Koethena, Lekthwa, Lenau, and Old Earth; also slaves of the races Byathid, Splang, Griffit, and Modok.

MAGDA a blue-green star orbited by a colonized world with five moons: Ista, Bista, Liad, Miad, and Poidel (WFM). Poidel is the fastest (closest) and Liad is the slowest (furthest).

MAGRA TARATEMPOS a hot white sun 30 l.y. from Old Earth, star of the planet of the Han (TEM).

HUMAN COLONISTS: 50,000.

AUTOCHTHONS: one million Han, pale humanoids worshiping the Great God Han. They sacrifice special gems to this god.

From this star system, Sol is between Sadal Suud and Sadal Melik in Aquarius, which makes it sound as though Magara Taratempos is located in the Leo constellation. This makes Denebola a candidate, being an A3 V star in Leo, 36 l.y. from Old Earth.

MAHA TRIAD a star system located between Magarak and Lenau (GI 6).

MAIL'S PLANET discovered by Kennes Mail (UR).

SURFACE AREA: .87 Earth.

GRAVITY: .93 g.

DIURNAL ROTATION: 22.15 hours.

YEAR: 2.97 Earth years.

CONTINENTS: One enormous equatorial continent, Gaea; three smaller subcontinents Atalanta, Persephone, and Alcyone.

MALLARD 42 a very Earth-like planet of the Commonwealth (TOB).

MALTASAR one of Nion's 19 moons.

MANGSTE a small world of a dim yellow star whose factories compete with the Druids of Kyril for regional economic dominance (ST 1). The Mang themselves are humans with lemon-yellow skin.

MARANIAN a world of the Alastor Cluster (Tr 4).

MARAPLEXA a yellow star located between Blue Star and Kay System (WB). The Kays call the star Melliflo. The Blues claim one of its planets, naming it "New Earth."

MARHAB star of planet "New Concept," said to be lemon-yellow and located in "the middle reaches of Aries" (BD 1). "Middle reaches" suggests it is rather far from Old Earth, "yellow" suggests it is a class G star. While the name sounds vexingly familiar (see MARKAB) there is no such named star in the constellation Aries. "Marhab(a)" is an Arabic word meaning "hello/welcome," suggesting it is a Vance coinage rather than a typo for "Markab."

Several candidates for this star in Aries are:

1. 51 Arietis, a G8 V star located 69 l.y. from Old Earth.
2. HD 20367, a G0 V star located 88 l.y. from Old Earth.
3. HIP 14810, a G5 V star located 172 l.y. from Old Earth.
4. BD +20°307, a G0 V star located 300 l.y. from Old Earth.
5. HAT-P-25, a G5 V star located 969 l.y. from Old Earth.

MARIAH a world of the Gaean Reach, sixth planet of white star Pfitz (POC 10.1).

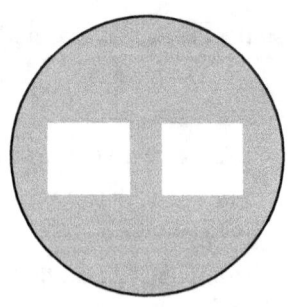

Slightly larger than Earth, it possesses a lower gravity due to lesser density. Four continents at regular intervals around equator:

- Alpha is bleak and rough, with four mountain ranges around a variety of deserts high and low. The spaceport town is Ascensor.
- Beta is located east of Gamma. Its blasted hills provide great mineral wealth. There is the suggestion of alien ruins. The Great Shinar Forest is home of the Klugash. The spaceport town is Cambria Town.
- Gamma is the largest, and frequently rainy. Its center has a vast swamp, drained by nine rivers. The spaceport town is Felker's Landing.
- Delta is the smallest and most charming, but it is surrounded by terrible sea-creatures of every size. Spaceport town is Sonc Town.

FOCUS ON FELKER'S LANDING OF GAMMA: Felker's Landing is situated at the brink of the Great Gorge of Gamma. The spaceport, at the eastern edge of town, also overlooks this gorge at a point where it is 500 feet wide and 200 feet deep. The "sprangs," a mesh of fragile walkways suspended from trusses extending over the Gorge, provide access to the kiki-nuts that grow on stalks rising from the swamp below. The river Amer flows down the center of Felker's Landing's main boulevard on its way to the Great Gorge.

Felker's Landing has a culture that uses color-coded ribbons (POC 11). A black headband is considered a mantle of invisibility—no one might notice a person who is wearing this. At puberty men wear blue-fringed headbands and women wear red-fringed headbands, henceforth oblivious to each other save as sexless blurs.

The north bank of the river Amer is considered female: visiting men must clip a small scarlet cockade to the bridges of their noses. Women must fix tufts of blue hair to their cheeks when they visit the south bank, usually when they wish to patronize one of the three taverns: the Prospero, the Black Tamber, or the Fazirab.

HISTORY OF MARIAH

Year	Event
25,000	Abel Mirklint discovers the planet.
26,000	Dondil Reske, age 13, leaves a few sketches in a book.
28,000	Fourteen statues are discovered in Great Shinar Forest near Cambria Town.

AUTOCHTHONS:

Klugash: Distant humans of Shinar forest, they are short, with slate colored skin, long thin legs, compact plump torsos, large pop-eyed heads crowned with a shock of gray-yellow bristles as stiff as quills (POC 10.2). The only ones seen are those who come out of the forest to beg at Cambria Town—all expeditions into the forest have been lost.

Arcts: Dragon-bat riding humans of the Gaspard Craigs of Gamma (POC 11). A child's sketchbook from 4,000 years ago depicts them, and they still exist. The Arcts prey upon the Yeltings, a related group living at the base of the Gaspards. Arct warriors capture Yelting women, and when these women no longer produce children, they work the crops in the high yards (POC 12.2).

Sea fauna of Delta (POC 10.2)

- Monitor-trapenoid, with eyestalks, tentacles, and man-eating jaws.
- Knife-fish, with razor sharp dorsal ridges.

- Nefring, with needle-noses.
- Gakkos, with heads like little sponges which, upon contact with human flesh, cause green festering.

MARKAB a highly developed star system in the Oikumene, it is noted for the "unbridled confusion" of its architecture (PL 3). "Markab" is an Arabic name historically applied to both Kappa Velorum, a B2 IV/V star located 450 l.y. from Old Earth, and Alpha Pegasi, a B9 V star located 160 l.y. from Old Earth.

MARKLAIDES a group of stars in the Polymark Cluster (LP 9).

MARMONFYRE planet of the Gaean Reach (DTA 8).

MARSKENS a world of the Oikumene (BD 9).

MARTIN CORDAS a name for star Andromeda 469, which see (MZ).

MARTINON'S FORT a high gravity world (HI 5).

MARUNE: ALASTOR 933 the horoscope world of the cluster (Ma). A planet of a four star system: orange dwarf Furad, blue dwarf Osmo, red dwarf Maddar, green star Cirse; located almost at the Cold Edge in the Fontinella Wisp.

A small dense world of no great population, Marune orbits Furad; Furad and Osmo orbit a common center; Maddar and Cirse orbit the Furad-Osmo system.

GEOGRAPHY: Rugged terrain; not a great deal of open water; vast equatorial bogs. Port Mar is the largest city (Ma 3); to the east are the Mountain Realms of the Rhune.

POPULATION:
- *Repulsed Invaders:* Rhunes.
- *Restored Colonists:* Majars.
- *Displaced Colonists:* A "lost" colony of 10,000 Majars in the low mountains south of Port Mar. A decadent and demoralized group slavishly affected by the modes.

- *Autochthons:* Fwai-chi. Wandering non-human pilgrims. Though lacking astronomy they can accurately predict modes far into the future. Travelers beware: they have memory-destroying drugs.

SOCIETY (RHUNE): The Rhunes, aloof and eccentric warrior-scholars, are culturally very serious and constrained. They have no music and are equally repulsed by issues of dining and sexual activity. They do, however, have a remarkable form of olfactory expression called "sherdas," an art of creating scent poems or symphonies by use of an odorifer (scent making device).

Marriage as such ("trisme") is strictly a political union; procreation is a byproduct of activities carried out only during mirk; since patrimony is often uncertain, rank and status derive from the mother. Aristocratic ranks of the Rhunes, from high to low: kaiark (king), kang (prince), eiodark (high ranking baron), baron, baronet, knight, and squire. Kraike (queen), lissolet (princess?), and wirwove are feminine ranks.

A Rhune's life-work is his Book of Deeds, which he writes, illustrates, and decorates with fervor and exactitude.

DIURNAL TIME RECKONING: Because of the elaborate orbits of the four local suns, Marune experiences true night (known as "mirk") only once every thirty days or so; the other days are each taken up with several different phases or "modes" randomly determined by the number of suns in the sky. Mirk is a time of madness, when all society's conventions and taboos are removed.

MODES OF MARUNE

	Furad	*Osmo*	*Madder*	*Cirse*
Aud	○	○	○	○
			Either	or both
Half-aud	○	○		
Isp		○	○	○
				With or
Chill isp		○		without
Umber	○		○	○
			Either	or both
Lorn umber	○			
Rowan			○	○
Red rowan			○	
Green rowan				○
Mirk				

THE EFFECTS OF MARUNE'S MODES UPON RHUNE SOCIAL BEHAVIOR

Mode	Rhune behavior
Aud	Study and practice; conflict (warfare, litigation, duel, collect rent).
Half-aud	Fresh, effervescent, and joyful.
Isp	Study and practice; formal ceremonies, including Ceremony of Odors.
Chill isp	Ascetic exultation.
Umber	Study and practice.
Lorn umber	(unknown)
Rowan	(unknown)
Red rowan	Slight relaxation of etiquette.
Green rowan	Poetry and sentimental musing.
Mirk	A time of rape, mayhem, and manslaughter.

(See also "Appendix VI: Notes on the Modes or Phases of Marune.")

TECHNOLOGY (RHUNE): Medieval level through technological proscription—by order of the Connatic, the Rhunes are forbidden to have energy weapons or high tech devices which could be used in warfare. This includes aircars, which Rhunes may hire as taxis at Port Mar but cannot own or drive themselves.

LAW (RHUNE): The distinction is made between mirk-deeds and premeditated murder.

CURRENCY: Ozol.

HISTORY: The original colonists were the Majars—the earliest name for the planet was "Majar-Rhune." The Rhunes made war upon the Majars until the Whelm expelled them to the eastern mountains and prohibited weaponry (Ma 3).

USEFUL TERMS:

Chorasm—sebalism carried to a remarkable degree.

Cogence—the fervent erudition and virtuosity of the Rhunes.

Low aud—aud just before the mode changes to umber.

Sebalism—the Rhune concept of sexuality, which they find disgusting.

Third Cycle—a time unit, perhaps equal to a season. See "Appendix VI: Notes on the Modes or Phases of Marune."

MASILIS an inhabited planet (NeP).

MASKE a self-isolated nature preserve world outside of the Gaean Reach (MT). Maske/Skay are double planets of the star Mora, located in the Great Hole beyond the Reach. Offworld traffic to and from Maske is forbidden: a local space patrol ensures compliance.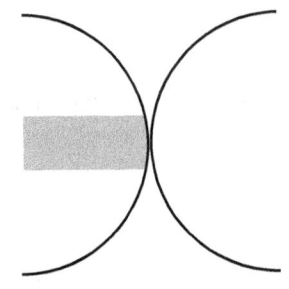

GEOGRAPHY: Maske has an equatorial ocean, "Long Ocean," with tides averaging forty feet (due to Skay). Thaery is the colonized territory and takes up a section of the northern litoral of the southern hemisphere.

GOVERNMENT: Anti-urban, anti-artificial. The semi-religious dictatorship of the original Gaean colonists has devolved over centuries into a bicameral parliament called The Parloury at Wysrod. The Landmoote represents the middle and lower castes, the Convention of Ilks represents the upper castes, and rule is by a group of four or five "Servants" elevated from noble houses. The real business of governing is handled by a meritocratic bureaucracy of six Departments (MT 6).

DEPARTMENTS OF THAERY

Department	Responsibility
D1	Maintains industrial safety.
D2	Controls price and quality standards.
D3	Sanitation and hygiene (and semi-secretly, espionage).
D4	Regulates weights and measures.
D5	Makes property evaluations.
D6	The Thariot Internal Police Force.

SOCIETY: The Thariots have various castes and clans; the Glints, an early dissident group, have been politically absorbed into Thaery but are still considered rustic and semi-barbarous; sea trade and travel is handled by the Sea Nationals (Glints); autochthonous peoples known as Djans (originally called Saidanese) are treated as slave laborers—their behavior depends largely upon how many Djan are in their immediate vicinity (the optimum number is four). The Djans weave rugs by hand, and these rugs are commonly ranked by the number of lifetimes taken to complete them: one-life, two-lives, etc.

DJAN WORK BY NUMBERS

Djan	Behavior
1	Performs aimlessly unless supervised.
2	Become intense; they either quarrel or fondle each other. Work suffers.
3	A disequilibrium; they work with agitation and resentful energy.
4	A stable system. They respond equably to orders but exert themselves only moderately and indulge themselves in comfort.
5	An unstable and dangerous combination. Four will presently form a group; the fifth, ejected, becomes resentful and bitter. He may go "solitary."
6	Yield one stable set and a pair of defiant lovers.
7	Create an unpredictable flux of shifting conditions and a turmoil of emotions.
8	After considerable shifting, conniving, testing, plotting, backbiting, yield two stable groups.

LAW: Thaery has a legal assassin guild, The Faithful Retribution Company. Warrants must be approved by a judge. Appeals can be made to arbitrators, but anticipated appeals can be officially denied in advance if noted on warrant.

EXPORTS: None, by definition (though Djan rugs might fetch a very good price offworld).

CURRENCY: Toldeck (planet wide only).

HISTORY: Colonists from Diosophede, a group of Credential Renunciators, found divergent humans already living on Maske and Skay. Of the fourteen ships, twelve formed a new compact upon arrival, a creed with two points—that a society would be established opposite to that of Diosophede's; and that the author of this compact would be hailed as a Triple Divinity. Twelve ships agreed to this, and each was granted a district; one ship agreed only to the first part, and was banished to the outlying rocky district called Glentlin; the remaining ship refused the compact and was shot down over wilderness on the northern continent—survivors reappeared as the Waels of Wellas, practicing strange druidical magics. After 300 years of skirmishing, Thaery occupied Glentlin. More centuries passed, and despite the Credential codes, some towns became cities.

USEFUL TERMS:

Ankhe—Sea National word for "malaise."

Culbrass—personal emblems, ornaments, tablets, and other insignia of ilk or caste, sometimes worn on dath. Used by noblemen.

Dath—a tall hat in the shape of a truncated cone.

Mais—marine glue with which all ships are built.

Nunciant—a formal speaker at the Parloury.

Perrupter—a Saidanese warrior (a solitary rogue Djan).

Quat—a flat four-cornered hat.

Yellow—time of freedom and carelessness, balanced by doing good deeds (weeding, road-repair, etc.) marking the transition between youth and maturity.

CRISIS: Conspirators want to introduce offworld tourism.

MAUBERLEY planet of the Gaean Reach (NL 14.1).

MAUDE white dwarf sun of Glory (DSB).

MAUDWELL'S STAR also known as Leo JN-44, its fifth planet is the Gaean Reach world Dimmick (POC 2.1).

MAURITAIN a populated world of the Terrestrial Empire (AC).

MAUVAISE an alien homeworld of giant worms (MMU).

MAXUS planet of slave-driven industry for 2,000 years (CM). It dominates the worlds of "the north end" of the Milky Way galaxy. Maxus has five moons. Its population is 40 million free Overmen, who are of Hyarnimmic ancestry (just like the Clas of Jena). Currency: Sil; a milray is a fraction of a sil.

MAZ a planet located at the border of three galactic nations: Gaean, Olefract, and Liss (DTA). An ancient Earth-like world orbiting star Khis.

ATMOSPHERE: Dense, with a curious smoky-orange nimbus.

SATELLITES: A large featureless moon.

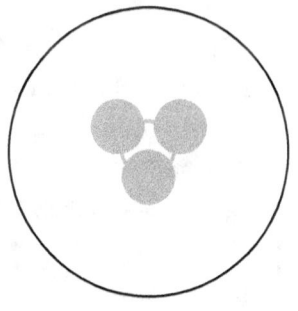

Axistil, Port of Maz

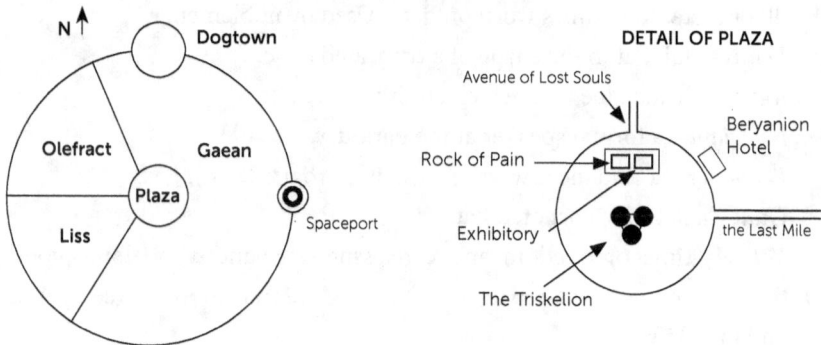

GEOGRAPHY: A dozen shallow seas and low ranges of hills, separated by swamps and sluggish rivers.

YEAR: 441 days (= 9587.34 hours).

DAY: 21.74 hours.

Axistil, the port city, is located somewhat north of the equator (DTA 3). The city has a circular plaza, beyond which it is divided into three adjoining sections: the Gaean sector, the Liss Sector, and the Olefract sector.

AUTOCHTHONS: The Gomaz, an intelligent, highly aggressive species. Discovered and armed by Geison Weirie, the Gomaz attempted to conquer the galaxy, attacking the Gaean, Liss, and Olefract nations.

The Gomaz are humanoid, with a white chitinous exoskeleton that serves as armor. Their weapons are few: a staff-mounted bola to trip the enemy; tongs; harpoons; and short heavy swords.

THE GOMAZ TYPES OF WAR	
Hate	A minority of wars fit this type.
Rivalry	Wars over economic necessity or territorial control.
Love	A type that is difficult to explain.

Culturally static for about a million years, the Gomaz are divided into 229 septs, each of which lives in a vast castle. They are monosexual, reproducing by planting zygotes into the body of a fallen warrior. Each individual is telepathically linked to all members of its sept. A juvenile is called a bantling and does all the work of a sept; the adults make war.

Year	Event
29,000	A "Hate" war between the Ubaikh, the Kzyk, and the Aqzh against the nomadic Hissau, formed the Steppe of Long Bones (DTA 10).
29,800	Kanitze sept wiped out by Ubaikh in a "Class III Rivalry War" (DTA 9).

Fauna

- Black angels.
- Gargoyles live in the mountains.
- Ixxen, blind white foxes that run in packs of 200 to 300.
- Flying snakes.

MAZDA a yellow star halfway along Mircea's Wisp, orbited by three hunks of rock and ice, and the planet Soum (Th 3.2).

MAZEN a planet (HI 6).

McDOODLE'S PLANET a possibly imaginary world of the Gaean Reach (Th 6.2).

McVANN'S STAR a star in Ophiuchus (PBD). During the era of the Tellurian Empire, prior to the Commonwealth, the planet here produced highly valued scented oils.

MEDELLIN a planet of the Commonwealth (KT).

MEL an alien inhabited world (MMU). These intelligent aliens are each eighteen feet long, with six big arms, a head something like a gorilla, and a thorax like a queen termite, all in the color of raw oysters. Each year on Mel lasts 14 Earth-years, and is divided into four "months" of 3.5 Earth-years each.

MELLIFLO the name used by the Kay for star Maraplexa (WB).

MENDASSIR a world where "sloebanks," forests of bushes, are found (CHO).

MERAKIN a planet of the Gaean Reach (Th 6.2).

MERCANTIL a world of the Polymark Cluster, inhabited by a society of traders doing business with 28 worlds of the cluster (LP 2).

METHEDEON a world of the Commonwealth (KW).

METHEL a world of the Oikumene (DP). Cora III; Argo Navis 961.

SATELLITES: One moon named "Shanitra" (after a grotesque clown in the Methlen opera bouffe).

GEOGRAPHY: A pleasant green world. Most of the planet is wilderness reserve. There is only one Methlen town (laid out more like an extended village), named Llalarkno, and a city (Twanish) for offworlders. The single spaceport is in Twanish—this and eight orbital forts help to keep Methel private and remote.

POPULATION:

- Methlen 20,000 in Llalarkno, 20,000 in country estates.
- Mongrels 50,000 in Twanish.

IMPORTED LABOR: Darsh and Mongrel (i.e., non-Darsh). The term "Mongrel" is not used by the Methlen but by the non-Darsh themselves as a sort of joke.

SOCIETY:

(Methlen): They are urbane bankers, hypersensitive to issues of status. Their dedication to rituals, pageants, tournaments, et cetera, proves that for Methlen, drama is more than just an art, it is a way of life. The term "Averroi" is an honorific.

(Mongrel): They imitate the Methlen even while they mock the Methlen for their excesses.

LAW: The most vile crime is unnatural sexual conduct.

EXPORTS: Capital; financial and management services.

CURRENCY: SVU.

HISTORY: Colonized by members of Aretioi, an exclusive club of Zangelberg on planet Stanislas (F 12).

METHUEN pink sun of Koryphon (GPr).

MIAD one of the five moons around the colonized world of star Magda (WFM).

MIEL a yellow star, the fifth planet of which is Sogdian (PL 9).

MIG binary with Pag, suns of Praesepe Three (NeP).

MILDRED'S BLUE WORLD a planet of the Gaean Reach, being a world beyond Mircea's Wisp (ArS 7.1).

MINTAKA SUB-30 star of Codiron (AbS). "Mintaka" is an old name for Delta Orionis, a star 900 l.y. from Old Earth.

MIRABILIS CLUSTER star group located between Halma and Old Earth (E 4; 19).

MIRACH the star of planet Koto, located in the Andromeda constellation (FGB 5). "Mirach" is an older name for Beta Andromedae, located 197 l.y. from Old Earth.

MIRALDA THE ENCHANTRESS a constellation seen from Koryphon, it contains the star Fenim (GPr 3).

MIRASSOU moon of Dar Sai (F 6).

MIRCEA'S WISP a structural feature of the Gaean Reach (ArS 1.1), with relevance to Andomeda 6011 IV, Aspergill, Caffin's World, Clarence Attic, Dauncy's World, Liliander's World, Mildred's Blue World, New Cavalry, Old Kharay, Old Lumas, Protagne, and Soum.

MIREILLE name of two different stars: the star of Sirene (MM); and the white-dwarf star of Star Home (Lu).

MIRIOTES an inhabited world of the Oikumene, the site of Farewell Station (F 12).

MIRSTEN a Gaean Reach planet near Blenkinsop (Lu 11.1). The city Falziel is on the single habitable continent where the coastal region is overgrown by forests of off-world and indigenous plants. Falziel is noted as a beautiful wooden city. Taverns here are marked with an effigy of Atlas. Export: precious woods.

MISH a blue-green moon of Gallingale (NL 8.4).

MIZAR Mizar; Ursa Major Sector; 83 l.y. from Old Earth. A nearby star system has planet Sirene (of "Moon Moth" fame).
- *Mizar's Third*—an inhabited world of the Oikumene (SK 6).
- *Mizar VI*—an Oikumene planet, home of a religious sect, the Tunkers (SK 7).

MONA a hot rockball of the Vega system (BD 8).

MONAGO the planet Taurus 61 III (HI 6).

MONTISERRA an inhabited planet famed for its floating cities (E 4).

MONTROY a Gaean Reach planet with an Institute of Transcendental Metaphysics (Lu 11.4).

MORA star of Skay/Maske, located in the Great Hole beyond the eastern fringe of the Gaean Reach (MT Preface).

MORBIHAN planet of the Gaean Reach "in back region of Aquila" (NL 10.4).

MORGAN a world orbiting the same star as Halma (E 4). A planet of wind-swept ocean, flat plateaus, and stark stone landscapes, it is the destination for tourists from Halma.

MORITABA a planet of the Commonwealth with a climate that is damp and unhealthy (KT). It orbits Pi Aquarii, which is 1,800 l.y. from Old Earth. Thievery here is a way of life, and the most successful becomes the king of thieves, ruler of the place.

MORLOCK a Gaean Reach planet of Argo Navis, with city Traven (Lu 3.4).

MOSSAMBEY a planet of the Gaean Reach (ArS 1.0).

MOTTRAM GROUP the star cluster that is home to Mazen (HI 10).

MOUDERVELT an Earth-like world of the Oikumene, the only populated planet of Van Kaathe's Star (BD 11).

Somewhat larger than Earth, it has a single continent sprawling two-thirds of the way around the equator. The world is old, its mountain ranges have eroded, leaving wide prairies. Fauna includes two-legged toad like creatures, lizard-foxes, and "cang," four inch stinging insects.

GOVERNMENT: Balkanized. Moudervelt has 1,562 separate dominions, each highly suspicious of the other. There are no true cities, but most of the lands have a spaceport.

FOCUS ON MAUNISH: Maunish, a dominion at the center of Goshen Prairie, has an area of 40,000 square miles and a population of one million, descended from a mission of the Pure Truth Partition. The principal town is Cloutie.

FOOD: "Maunce" is an entrée of river-fish and herbs. Beverages are strictly non-alcoholic due to religious proscription, leading to such drinks as chilled gruel seepings, tanglefoot soak, kidney tonic, nibbet (a vitalizing tea), soursap toddy, and belchberry sprig.

Still, members of the upper class scandalously enjoy alcohol in public, drinking such spirits as Nectar of Phlox, Blue Tears, Now-You-See-Me, and Ammary.

RELIGIOUS FIGURES:

- *Didram Bandervoum*—his statue holds aloft a carpenter's try-square that he might gauge the souls of the dead.
- *Didram Bodo Sime*—he penned obloquies against the Toper and his drink.
- *Didram Runel Fluter*—his statue holds in one hand a short curved knife and in the other a severed set of male genitalia.

USEFUL MAUNISH TERMS:

Bewalkus—buttocks.

Counterwink—to go against.

Didram—church leader.

Marmelizer—a type of undertaker who creates memorial statues from the bodies of the dead.

Marmel—a corpse-statue at a cemetery.

Sanivacity—the health-giving, nourishing quality of fruit, in contrast to the fruit decayed into alcohol.

Toper—a Teaching term for the drunkard.

Valetudinarian—a strict tee-totaler for religious reasons, from a real word for a person who is unduly anxious about his health.

Vardespant—"indecorous," colored with notions of obstinancy, perverse wrong-headedness, a jeering attitude toward somber rectitude.

Werd—a man-shaped supernatural being who prowls by night. According to Maunish folklore, it hides in the shadows, waiting to pounce on children and carry them away.

MOULDER 17 see BLENKINSOP.

MOULTON'S WORLD an inhabited world of the Gaean Reach, the deportation site for Yips found living illegally on Cadwal's Deucas (ArS 4.4).

MOUNT PLEASANT an agricultural settlement on Providence, a world of the Beyond (BD 1). It had a population of 5,000, all of whom were enslaved in the raid of the combined Demon Princes in the year 1499 (SK 10).

MU ANDROMEDAE an inhabited star system (MZ).

MUGH an inhabited world of the Commonwealth (SSS).

MUR the sun of Zeck in the Alastor Cluster (W 2).

MURCHISON solitary planet of Murchison's Star in the Beyond, site of slave-operated tapestry factories (PL 3). Single big continent circling the equator. The Bower Mountain aborigines are black natives who are hunted for sport.

MURCHISON'S STAR also known as Sagitta 203, located in Sagitta Sector, 30 l.y. beyond the Pale (PL 3).

MURTSEY a planet of the Gaean Reach (NL 14.3).

N

NAHARIUS a planet of the Gaean Reach located at Virgo GGP 922, in the Pergola Region of space (POC 1.7).

The population is relatively sparse, concentrated in Trajence, a partially urbanized settlement next to the spaceport. A few miles east of Trajence is Mount Maldoun, an extinct volcano among low hills. Down the mountainside flow three streams that become charged, according to local beliefs, with remarkable powers. Even more potent are the waters from the sacred springs at the base of the mountain (Lu 12.2).

NAOS a yellow star of the Commonwealth with two inhabited planets (HB). "Naos" is an old name for Zeta Puppis, found 2,100 l.y. from Old Earth.
- *Naos V*—one of the most pleasant planets of the Commonwealth.
- *Naos VI*—the only planet where ticholama, source of resilian, is grown.

NARFILHET original homeworld of the exile Laoome (WT).

NATRICE a planet of Blaise, a blue star of the Gaean Reach (CAD).

PHYSICAL: Modest size, small polar ice caps, dense atmosphere.

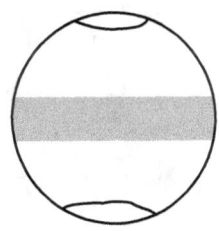

GEOGRAPHY: Hemispheres roughly symmetrical, separated by a narrow equatorial sea, the Mirling. The northern hemisphere is the Lanklands. Cities face each other across Mirling: Poinciana, the largest (spaceport), Halcyon.

HISTORY: The first colonists arrived while Natrice still lay "Beyond." Retired pirates, slavers, fugitives, and ordinary criminals established comfortable estates along the shores of the Mirling and became the Patrunes of Natrice. Centuries passed. The Reach expanded and a wave of Sanart Scientists (over one million naturopathic philosophers) settled the Lanklands (ArS 7).

CURRENCY: Sol.

NAUTILUS a circlet of five white stars seen in the southern sky of Cadwell, with Sol at its center (ArS 6.2).

NEKKAR IV a Commonwealth world (SJA). "Nekkar" is an Arabic name for Beta Boötis, located 225 l.y. from Old Earth.

NEROLI an inhabited world of the Gaean Reach (FT 1).

NEW ACQUITAIN an important Commonwealth planet (KT). See STARPORT.

NEW CALVARY a planet of Mircea's Wisp (ArS 7.1).

NEW CONCEPT a world of the Oikumene (DP). Marhab VI, Aries sector.

SATELLITES: Three moons (BD 1).

New Concept was originally colonized by strict vegetarian humans who, by the year 1500, had long since seemingly devolved into fleet-footed grazers known as Feeks (BD 1; 2). Human residents use domesticated Feeks as house servants.

ARTS: The original settlers created many beautiful things, including the Gongs of New Concept, the best of which were hidden in caves (BD 2).

CURRENCY: SVU.

NEW EARTH a planet of Maraplexa, claimed by Blue Star and named in an allusion to long-lost Old Earth (WB). While many of the physical details are Earth-like, there is no life and the atmosphere is pre-organic, so the Blues begin a project to transform the atmosphere. In the end, New Earth might be Old Earth, after all.

NEW GORCHERUM Oikumene world (BD 9).

NEW HELLAS a world settled after the invention of the Langtry space-drive (FGB 7). The mutated humans here are the long-limbed Hepetanthroids.

NEW HOPE a world of the Beyond (SK 9). Possibly the same as the Gaean Reach world with city Croy, out by Fluter (Lu 9.7).

NEW OSSINING the prison world that the Two Hundred were being sent to when they escaped to Blue World (BW 2). However, there is also a city named New Ossining on the planet Olliphane of the Rigel Concourse (SK 5), raising the possibility that the two are one and the same.

NEW SUDAN an Earth-like planet of the Commonwealth (TOB).

NIGHT LAMP a vagabond star located in the intergalactic gulf beyond the fringe of the Milky Way (NL 13.6). It is a yellow-white dwarf with four planets, including Fader.

NILO-MAY the single planet of Yellow Rose star located at the edge of the Gaean Reach (NL).
GEOGRAPHY: Equatorial desert.
POPULATION: Three thousand human colonists living in town/space-port Loorie. Quietly engaged in monopolistic trade with the otherwise lost world of Fader (NL 13).
HISTORY: Located originally by the legendary Wilbur Wailey (see SAFRONILLA).
CURRENCY: Sol.

NINKA one of Nion's 19 moons.

NION a planet of the Gaean Reach (CAD). Pharisse VI, a world with 19 moons (EOE 8.3).

> DIAMETER: 13,000 miles.
>
> GRAVITY: 1.03.
>
> MEAN DAY: 37.26 hours.
>
> SATELLITES: Nineteen moons, including Garuun, Lilimel, Maltasar, Ninka, Padan, Res, Seis, Shan, Sigil, and Zosmei.
>
> GEOGRAPHY: Tanjaree is the single large city and spaceport.
>
> FRINGE SOCIETY: Planetary Engineers work at improving the plateaus with flora from Old Earth. Another group, the Shadowmen, is obsessive about the moons in the sky (EOE 9.2; 9.3).

NOAILLE one of Vega's three inner worlds, it has rains of liquid mercury (BD 8).

NOIR dark star that orbits binary pair Rouge and Blanche, passing close to planet Jexjeka (TOB).

NONESTIC GULF a boundary of the Alastor Cluster (W 1).

NOPALGARTH the homeworld of nopals (NOP). BXOQE, as it turns out.

NOVA BACTRIA a world of the Oikumene (BD 4).

NOVAL an important planet of the Oikumene (SK 3). Location unknown.

NOVO MUNDO an inhabited world (FGB 4).

NOWHERE a world of the Rigel Concourse, home to the Lenka who are famous for their workmanship in crafting panels in bone, shell, and wood (PL 4).

NUMENES the capital world of Alastor Cluster, presumably "Alastor 1" (Ma). Planet Blazon ("Alastor 2"?) next orbit out from Numenes.

GEOGRAPHY: Numenes has islands but no real continents (Ma 2). The Connatic's Palace has a vast museum called the Ring of Worlds, which has a separate display for each world of the Cluster.

CURRENCY: Ozol.

NUMOY a planet of the Gaean Reach (POC 8.1).

ODFARS fourteenth world of Sigma Sculptoris (TLJ). A cold, vacuum world with lakes of quicksilver. This star is located 227 l.y. from Old Earth.

OIKUMENE named after a Greek word meaning "the known world," the Oikumene is an interstellar nation of more than ninety inhabited planets (SK 3), probably the precursor to the Gaean Reach. Occupying a bubble of space perhaps 2,000 l.y. around Earth, outside of which lies "the Beyond." Three powerful groups have influence in the Oikumene: the Institute (academics and scientists), the Jarnell Corporation (stardrive manufacture), and the IPCC (Interworld Police Coordination Company). The Beyond is the area of pirates, outlaws, and the Deweaseling Brigade, a group set on killing IPCC agents.

COSMOPOLITAN WORLDS OF THE OIKUMENE	
World(s)	*Star*
Alphanor, Krokinole, Olliphane	Rigel
Cuthbert, Boniface, Aloysius	Vega
Noval	(unknown)
Copus, Orpo	Pi Cassiopeiae
Quantique	Alphard
Old Earth	Sol

DISTANCE BETWEEN STARS (IN L.Y.)

	Sol	Vega	Pi Cas	Alphard
Vega	25	0		
Pi Cas	174	164	0	
Alphard	177	195	310	0
Rigel	860	880	852	796

CALENDAR: The Oikumene uses the standard English language calendar of twelve months.

RELIGION: The Oikumene seems to recognize 13 different supreme deities, among them "Kalzibah," "Syarasis," and possibly "Jehu" and "Symas." Oikumene devils include "Sclamoth," who puts the heads of sons in their mother's ovens (F 7).

SKIN TONES: Fashionable citizens use a full spectrum of body paints (for example yellow, black, dark-buff, satin-green, blue, beige, white, sallow, russet, purplish-maroon). A certain blue-brown tone was originally thought to protect the human organism from certain mysterious Jarnell effluviae, and became a standard for travel (SK 9).

SPORTS/HOBBIES: There is "kalingo," which seems to be a sport or a hobby (KM 8).

CURRENCY: The SVU, Standard Value Unit.

PLANETS OF THE OIKUMENE: Algenib IX, Aloysius, Alphanor, Alphard VI, Alpheratz VI, Arcturus IV, Barleycorn, Bernal, Bethune Preserve, Bogardus, Boniface, Brinktown, Canopus III, Capella VI, Caph IV, Chrysanthe, Copus, Cuenos Notos, Cuthbert, Cytherea Tempestre, Dar Sai, David Alexander's Planet, Derdyra, Diogenes, Dubhe, Duptis Major, Elfland, Espandencia, Euville, Fiame, Ghnarumen, Goshen, Green Star, Hardacres, Hyaspis, Idora, Image, Irta, Jezebel, Killarney, Krokinole, Lorgan, Lupus 23 II, Lyonnesse, Madagascar, Marhab, Markab, Marskens, Methel, Miriotes, Mizar VI, Mizar's Third, Mona, Moudervelt, New Concept, New Gorcherum, Noaille, Nova Bactria, Noval, Nowhere, Olam, Old Earth, Olliphane, Orpo, Padraic, Pilgham, Quantique, Quinine, Raratonga, Reis, Sadal Suud Four, Sandusk, Sardanipoli, Sarkovy, Sirene, Somewhere, Spica VI, Stanislas, Tantamount, Terranova, Tertulian, Unicorn, Vadilov, Vale, Valhalla, Valisande, Vanello, Verlaren, Walpurgis, Wirfil, Xion, Yellow Sun Planet, Ys, and Zacaranda.

OLAM an Oikumene world known to have living jewels (SK 11).

OLANTHUS single moon of Scropus (POC 4.3).

OLD EARTH Sol III

Old Earth of the Oikumene (circa year 1524).
Asia
- Sinkiang, a city with resorts (PL 7).

Africa
- The Sahara Sea (PL 7).

Europe
- Ambeules, a suburb of Rolingshaven on the west coast of Europe (PL 3) is on the Gaas (PL 3).
- Rolingshaven: Gaas River and Sluicht River, great Evres Canal (PL 4).
- West Europe spaceport at Tam (PL 3).
- London by tube (PL 4).
- Wien, Paris, Tsargrad, Berlin, Budapest, Kiev, Neapolis, Amsterdam (PL 4).

North America
- Edmonton, Canada, is the Holy City of Kalzibah (PL 9). Hordes of pilgrims come to gaze upon the Sacred Shin.
- Oakland (BD 3).
- Philadelphia (BD 4).

Old Earth of the Gaean Reach (circa year 30,000).
North America
- The Big Prairie (EOE prologue).
- Idola, a town on Big Prairie.

Europe
- Ambeules, on western end of continent (EOE 7.1).

The Balkans
- Shillawy is located far to the southwest of Kiev, which seems to put it in the Balkans (EOE 5.3). Situated on the River Taing (EOE 4.2), it features the Grand Fiamurjes Spaceport and the Library of Ancient Archives (EOE 3.1). Fifty miles south of Shillawy is the

manor Fair Winds at the hamlet Yssinges near the village Tierans (EOE 3.1). Shillawy might be around the area of historical Sofia.

- Sancelade is a city 200 miles NW of Fair Winds (EOE 3.5). History of Sancelade (EOE 4.1). Sancelade might be around the area of Belgrade, if Shillawy is analogous to Sofia.
- Great Transylvanian Preserve mentioned (EOE 3.1).
- Zagreb mentioned (EOE 6).

Ukraine
- Kiev (EOE 3.1). Not far from Kiev is the town Draczeny in the Moholc, location of castle Mirky Porod (EOE 6.1).
- Croy city might be in Ukraine (EOE 5.3).
- Ybarra spaceport seems to be in Ukraine (EOE 5.5).

Old Earth of The Last Castle *(in the Post Gaean Reach period).*

NINE CASTLES: Halcyon, Delora, Morninglight, Tuang, Sea Island, Maraval, Alume, Janeil, and Hagedorn (LC 2). Hagedorn located near Lucerne Valley.

TRANSPORTATION: Living Powerwagons for land travel, talkative and surly Birds (group will carry a passenger on a chair) for air travel. (Note: "syrup" is the food source for Phanes, Peasants, Meks, Powerwagons, and Birds.)

POPULATION:

Castle dwellers
- *Aristocracy*—Gentlemen and ladies, descendants of humans from Altair.
- *Imported beauties*—Phanes, pretty creatures from moon of Albireo VII (LC 4). Cultivated by the Gentlemen but not sexually engaged without scandal.
- *Imported farmers*—Peasants, small andromorphs originally from Spica X (LC 2).
- *Imported laborers*—Meks, native to planet Etamin IX (LC 1.3).

Non-Castle dwellers
- *Expiationists*—humans who left the castles to form villages.
- *Nomads*—humans who migrate and claim to be autochthonous rather than descended from Altaireans. Usually at odds with the Castle dwellers, stealing, vandalizing, and fighting skirmishes.

CRISIS: The plan to repatriate imported labor triggers Mek uprising.

OLD KHARAY a planet of the Gaean Reach famous for its exotic canals (ArS 1.6).

OLD LUMAS a planet of Mircea's Wisp (ArS 7.1).

OLEFRACT ⚑ an alien interstellar nation, contemporary to the Gaean Reach (DTA). See also LISS.

OLFANE a Gaean Reach planet of Sigil 92 (Lu 3.4).

OLLIPHANE a cosmopolitan world of the Oikumene (SK 3). Located close at the outer edge of Rigel's Habitable Zone (SK 5). Rigel Concourse planet number 19; Orion Sector; 860 l.y. from Old Earth.

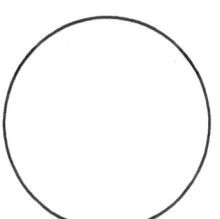

DIAMETER: 6,700 miles.

MASS: 0.9. With the highest density of the Rigel planets, Olliphane is relatively cool and wet.

POPULATION: The Olphs are a mingled stock, derived primarily from a colony of Hyperborean Skakers. The population is concentrated in the Equatorial Zone, especially around the shores of Lake Clare.

SOCIETY: The most highly industrialized planet of the Concourse, with a diligent and disciplined workforce. A caste system permeates every phase of the social structure.

GOVERNMENT: Balkanized, with nineteen independent nations, including Braichis (SK 3).

CURRENCY: SVU.

OLOE large moon of Maz.

OMICRON CETI III an Earth-like planet of the Commonwealth (TOB). Omicron Ceti is located 170 l.y. from Old Earth.

OPHIR a Commonwealth world, one of only two where telex is mined (KT). The other world is Moritaba.

OPHIUCHUS a region of the Gaean Reach (NL 1.1).

ORPHEUS a constellation seen from Koryphon (GPr 3). The figure's lute is composed of eight blue stars.

ORPO Pi Cassiopeiae VII, a cosmopolitan world of the Oikumene, it orbits Pi Cassiopeiae along with Copus (KM 2).

ORVIL a world at the edge of the Gaean Reach (Th 6.3).

OSMO blue dwarf star of Marune in Alastor Cluster (Ma 3). Orbited by dead worlds Haune and Douaune.

P

PADAN one of Nion's 19 moons.

PADME a world of the Commonwealth far away from Hither Sagittarius (CG).

PADRAIC a scorched inner planet of the Vega system (BD 8).

PAG with Mig, one of Praesepe Three's twin suns (NeP).

PAGHORN a planet in the Aries sector of the Gaean Reach (NL 13.2).

PALO a world of the Beyond (KM 2).

PANAPOL an inhabited planet (ST 3).

PANDORA a world of the Commonwealth (SSS).

PANDORA CHROMATICS a group of stars or planets in the Gaean Reach (NL 12.6).

PANGBORN a world where human lords fight each other with magic and technology, and autochthons get in the way (MW).

STAR: Large, pale, and faintly pink.

AUTOCHTHONS: "First Folk," driven from the downs into the forests 1,600 years ago. They have chitinous heads, enormous hands with chisel-fingers, multifaceted big black bug eyes, and they express protective foam from under their arms.

- *Technology:* They use wasp guns, make traps (pit, scythe, and deadfall).
- *Magic:* They can cause forests to grow up from nothing overnight.

HUMANS: Human space captains, their home bases destroyed, took refuge on Pangborn and pushed the First Folk into the forests.

- *Technology:* Medieval level, augmented with failing heirlooms of long lost technology (fliers, energy pistols, and starship cannons).
- *Magic:* Magic-using "Jinxmen" practicing a blend of "hoodoo," including voodoo dolls, demon conjuring, demonic inspiration, telepathy, telepathic suggestion, and teleportation.

DEMONOLOGY

Name	Power
Pont	Sleep
Deigne	Fear
Everid	Wrath
Keyril	?
Dant	?

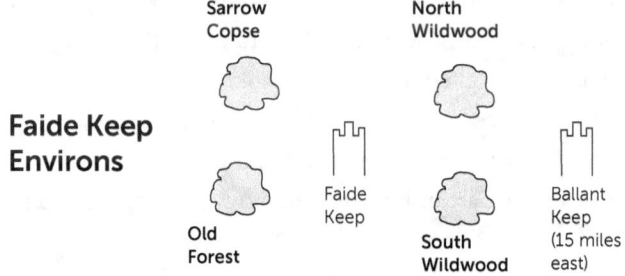

Faide Keep Environs

Sarrow Copse

North Wildwood

Old Forest

Faide Keep

South Wildwood

Ballant Keep (15 miles east)

PAO a planet of Auriol, a type G star in the Polymark Cluster (LP).

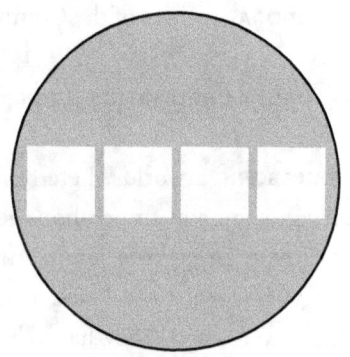

DIAMETER: 11,006 miles.

MASS: 1.73 earths.

GRAVITY: 1.04 g.

AXIAL TILT: 0° (no seasons).

GEOGRAPHY: Eight continents range the equator, named after the eight digits of the Paonese numerative system: Aimand (largest), Shraimand, Vidamand (growers of grapes and fruit), Minamand (with capital city Eiljanre), Nonamand (smallest, having one-fourth the area of Aimand; it also suffers an unpleasant climate as it is located in the high southern latitudes), Dronamand, Hivand (featureless expanse), and Impland.

POPULATION: 15 billion (human), mainly living in country villages.

INVADERS: The Brumbos (human) of Batmarsh, a small planet three stars away from Pao (LP 8).

GOVERNMENT: Absolute monarchy by the Panarch, hereditary ruler.

SOCIETY: For 5,000 years Pao had been homogenous but somewhat inefficient; exploited by crafty traders, technologically backward, prone to famine, an easy target for invaders.

In an attempt to alter the society as quickly as possible (in years rather than decades), scientists at Breakness Institute (another world) devised a number of synthetic specialized languages: Valiant (warriors), Technicant (merchants), and Cogitant (scholars), to be used in addition to Pao (non-specialists). This linguistic division required the creation of an additional caste of interpreters to facilitate communication between all castes. While in some ways the experiment was a great success, undesirable side-effects among the Paonese, as well as rapacious behavior by Institute representatives, brought it to a close. In the effort to reknit the social fabric, Pastiche (a new language patched together half-jokingly by the trainee interpreters) will probably become the new common language.

LAW: "Subaqueate" means to execute by drowning.

ARTS: Competitive sports are unknown. Ceremonial chanting ("drones") in groups of ten to twenty million.

EXPORT: Trade with planet Mercantil.

CALENDAR: Every eighth day is market day; every sixty-fourth day is a drone day; every 512th day is a continental fair day (LP 9).

PAONESE POPULATIONS BY CONTINENT

Continent	Notes
Aimand	-
Shraimand	Warrior caste/Valiant language during experiment.
Vidamand	Locals said to be large hearted and expansive; location of Industry and Merchant caste/Technicant language.
Minamand	Locals considered urbane and frivolous.
Nonamand	Locals said to possess dour thrift and fortitude; home of scholar caste/Cogitant language during experiment.
Dronamand	-
Hivand	Locals considered exemplars of bucolic naivete.
Impland	-

PEGASUS KE58 the white star commonly known in the Gaean Reach as Tyr Gog (Th 4.2). Orbited by Rhea, six small rocky worlds, a gas giant, and an ice world. This star might be 58 Pegasi, a B9 III star found 619 l.y. from Old Earth.

PEGASUS RECTANGLE a region of space, wherein the Gaean Reach planet Rosalia is located (ArS 1.4), and possibly the world Procrustes (SU). Presumably this is the rectangle in the constellation Pegasus formed by Alpha Pegasi, Gamma Pegasi, Beta Pegasi, and Alpha Andromedae.

PENTADEX a constellation seen from Koryphon (GPr 8).

PENTAGRAM a constellation of the Alastor Cluster, located between Numenes and the Fontinella Wisp (Ma 4); a strangely regular constellation of the Gaean Reach seen from Araminta Station (ArS 4.5).

PERDU a highly ranked world raided by the Klau (GI 14).

PERGOLA REGION a part or sector of space that contains Scropus, Fluter, Blenkinsop, Kyril, and Naharius (POC 4.1). (A pergola is a shaded walkway in a garden or arbor.)

PERKINS an inhabited planet where Ballenkart slaves are used as bodyguards (ST 10).

PERSEIAN LIMBO an area of space far beyond the civilized worlds of mankind (FGB 4). Presumably it is located in the constellation Perseus.

PERSEID ARM a feature of the Milky Way galaxy, an arm of stars located toward the galactic rim from Old Earth, situated in the Orion Arm. Between these arms is a relatively empty region, a gap or gulf.

PERSEUS HOLDING HIGH THE HEAD OF MEDUSA a constellation seen from Cadwal, wherein Cairre and Aquin form the eyes of Medusa (ArS 6.2). This is probably not our constellation Perseus, since ours holds the head of Medusa rather low, and the name of this one sounds more like Benvenuto Cellini's famous bronze statue "Perseus with the Head of Medusa" (A.D. 1545). Our constellation has Algol, with a name suggesting it is the eye of a monster; whereas this one has two eyes.

PERSEUS TT-652-IV a Gaean Reach planet called Kars, orbiting a star in the Perseus sector (Th 6.6).

PERSIGIAN Auriga 225-G, or perhaps Leo 4A563 (MMU). Alien inhabited system, where the aliens look like bright blue lizards and sting like nettles upon contact.

PEST-HOLE a planet of griffins (AbS).

PFITZ STAR a white sun orbited by Mariah (POC 10.1). Discovered by Abel Merklint, it was originally named "Laura Ardelia Pfitz."

PHAEDRA star with four worlds, the innermost being the low-density Big Planet, the remaining three being very dense (BP 1).

PHALID homeworld of the Phalid, located at an insignificant star in Lyra (PF 6). The Phalid are a race of spacefaring humanoids with insect-like attributes. Travel to the world from Tellurian Earth takes three weeks. Phalid reproduction involves symbiotic union between Phalid and an intelligent plant.

PHARIS: ALASTOR 458 a world of the Alastor Cluster (W 8).

PHARISSE Nion's sun, Argo Navis 14-AR-366, a yellow-white star of the Gaean Reach (EOE 8.2).
- *Pharisse VI*—the inhabited planet Nion.

PHARISTANE an inhabited planet of the Gaean Reach (GPr 6).

PHARODE a planet of the Beyond (SK 2).

PHASIS a planet of the Gaean Reach, located in the Aries sector (NL 13.2).

PHI OPHIUCHI star of the Oikumene (SK 4). See SARKOVY.

PHI ORIONIS star of planet Zade (SO). There are two stars with this name, one that is 120 l.y. from Old Earth (Phi Ori-1), the other being 1000 l.y. away (Phi Ori-2).

PHOCAN'S CAULDRON a cluster of blue and white stars seen from Blue World (BW 3).

PHRENESIAN BLACKNESS an empty region of space in Tellurian/Commonwealth sphere (PBD).

PHRIST a planet of the Gaean Reach (MT 9).

PI AQUARII a star of the Commonwealth, it is located 1,800 l.y. from Old Earth (KT).

PI CASSIOPEIA star, 174 l.y. from Old Earth. Properly Pi Cassiopeiae.
- *Pi Cassiopeiae VII*—Oikumene world Orpo (KM 2).
- *Pi Cassiopeiae VIII*—Oikumene world Copus (SK 3).

PI SAGITTARIUS star of Kokod (KW). Properly Pi Sagittarii, it is located 310 l.y. from Old Earth.

PILGHAM a world of the Rigel Concourse (SK 4). The name is unique among them, and subsequently mysterious.

PLAIS Alschain XIV is inhabited by aliens, small humanoids looking like big-eyed elves, having eyebrows of green feathers and hair that is as thin and pale as corn-silk (MMU). They are insectivorous.

PLAISE a Gaean Reach planet not far from the edge of the galaxy, settled during the first great expansion of humanity into the stars (NL 3.1).

PLANET OF THE BLACK DUST an inhabited world orbiting a red star in the Serpens group, it is about half the size of Earth (PBD). The green-tinted atmosphere is breathable but tainted with poisons a filter mask can stop. Authochthons are 15-feet tall and vaguely humanoid.

POIDEL fastest of the five moons orbiting Magda's planet (WFM).

POLARIS a planet (ST 9). Presumably at the star of that name, in Ursa Minor. Polaris is located 434 l.y. from Old Earth.

POLENSIS a world where mercenary troops may be hired (LP 9).

POLYMARK CLUSTER a star group containing Batmarsh, Breakness, Hallow-mede, Journal, Mercantil, Pao, Polensis, and Vale (LP 1).

POLYMARKS a group of stars in the Gaean Reach, perhaps referring to the Polymark Cluster (NL 12.6).

POLYPOLIS city of Old Earth, it seems to be the capital of the Home Planets (MM).

PORPHYRITE the Druid name for a constellation seen from Kyril (ST 2).

PORRIDGE POT a dark nebula near Spica (BP 3).

PORTMAR'S PLANET alien homeworld where the autochthons are akin to centipedes (UM).

PRAESEPE THREE a human-inhabited planet of the twin pink stars Mig and Pag (NeP). The dead city Therlatch in the desert, a thousand years abandoned, has a number of large public buildings: the Legalic (Hall of Records and Decisions), the Mosque, the Hall of Relicts, and the Sumptuar. The Sumptuar at first glance appears to be a temple of holy maidens (like the vestal virgins), but it seems more like a civic brothel of temple prostitutes. (Note that while "Praesepe" is a valid astronomical name, it refers to an entire cluster, the Beehive Cluster in Cancer, rather than a single star.)

PRANILLA a Gaean Reach world with extraordinary sunsets (EOE 3.3).

PRIMARCHIC ⚑ an interstellar nation beyond both the Alastor Cluster and the Gaean Reach (Tr prolog). A grouping of stars somewhat smaller than the Alastor Cluster, at one time controlled by the Primarch, but later in a chronic state of disorder, factionalism, and war. Protecting the Alastor Cluster against raids from the Primarchic is an important function of the Connatic's Whelm (W 10).

PROCRUSTES inhabited world with two suns, one red and the other blue-white (SU). The currency is the Juillard crown. The local newspaper is "The Pegasus Square Farm and Mining Bulletin," suggesting that the star is located in the Pegasus Rectangle, or that the city's name is "Pegasus Square" (*An Encyclopedia of Jack Vance* entry on "Pegasus Square"), or perhaps even both.

PROCYON name of star Alpha Canis Minoris, located in Canis Minor Sector, 12 l.y. from Old Earth.

- *Procyon*—an inhabited world (SO 1).

- *Procyon*—where the intelligent autochthons each look like forty feet of thick cable (MMU).
- *Procyon B*—a world with sparkle-ticks (WLA).

PROSPERUS the star of world Akhabats (FGB 1).

PROTAGNE a Gaean Reach planet of Mircea's Wisp (ArS 7.1).

PROVIDENCE a planet in the Beyond near Ferrier's Cluster, the site of Mount Pleasant (BD 1). Like planet Grabhorne, it is in the area of space once claimed by Malagate the Woe.

PTERNI an inhabited world (GI 4).

PURLOPPAT an industrial planet of the Klau (GI 20).

PUSKOLITH a colonized planet (CHO).

Q

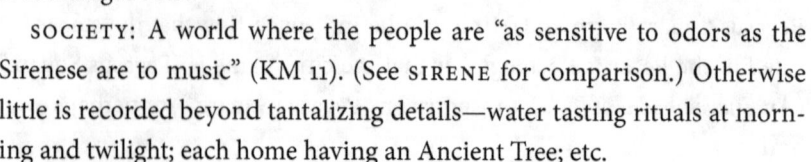

QUANTIQUE a cosmopolitan world of the Oikumene (SK 3); sixth planet of Alphard the Lonely (KM 2). Alphard VI; Hydra Sector; 177 l.y. from Old Earth.

GEOGRAPHY: Pamfile city of Zaccare region has a hundred perfume manufactories. Near Pamfile is Talalangi Forest.

SOCIETY: A world where the people are "as sensitive to odors as the Sirenese are to music" (KM 11). (See SIRENE for comparison.) Otherwise little is recorded beyond tantalizing details—water tasting rituals at morning and twilight; each home having an Ancient Tree; etc.

RELIGION: The god-yell, at the following times: morning, evening, "rogue," and "unpremeditated." Each situation requiring a different scent.

EXPORTS: Perfumes.

CURRENCY: SVU.

QUINCUNX a constellation in the Gaean Reach, across the Great Hole from Maske (MT 9).

QUININE a planet of the Rigel Concourse (SK 4).

R

RAMPOLD a world being tamed for colonization (AC). Fauna includes atrachids, mammoth amphibious creatures.

RAMUS a giant red star, sun of Fell (CM).

RARATONGA a world of the Rigel Concourse (SK 4). After the Pacific island Rarotonga, capital of the Cook Islands on Old Earth.

REIS Oikumene planet Gamma Eridani VI; Eridanus Sector; 150 l.y. from Old Earth (F 3).

RES one of Nion's 19 moons.

RESURGE a planet with a penal colony, very distant from Old Earth of the Terrestrial Empire (AC).

RHAMNOTIS: ALASTOR 965 a world so excellently managed that the optimums have become norms (Tr 3). A place where the Tamarchô ("Ugly People") rebel against the perfection by deliberately fouling their world.

RHEA sole inhabited world of Tyr Gog in Pegasus (CAD). A planet of the Gaean Reach.
A small, dense planet rich in exotic minerals, Rhea has two large continents (Myrdal and Wrake), a canted orbit, retrograde rotation, and an asymmetric shape (Th 4). Wrake has mining and industry, while to the south, Myrdel is reserved for the estates of the Twelve Families.

RHO OPHIUCHUS IV sulfur planet in a double-star system, with a large orange star, a yellow star, and four planets (SSP). Properly Rho Ophiuchi, the system is located 400 l.y. from Old Earth.

SIZE: Smaller than Earth.

ATMOSPHERE: An oily yellow mix of hydrogen sulfide, sulfur dioxide, SO_3, oxygen, and halogen acids.

AUTOCHTHONS: "Fuzz-balls," yellow creatures looking like a blend of barrel cactus and sea urchin, four feet tall and two feet thick. Each one works for one of the many castles.

RHODOPE also known as Fomalhaut IV, a planet of the Commonwealth (SSS). One of the more Earth-like planets of the Commonwealth (TOB).

RIGEL a star, also known as Beta Orionis, located 860 l.y. from Old Earth and host to the Rigel Concourse: Alphanor (capital world, Rigel VIII), Barleycorn, Chrysanthe, Diogenes, Elfland, Fiame, Goshen, Hardacres, Image, Jezebel, Krokinole (Rigel XIV), Lyonnesse, Madagascar, Nowhere, Olliphane (Rigel XIX), Pilgham, Quinine, Raratonga, Somewhere, Tantamount, Unicorn, Valisande, Walpurgis, Xion, Ys, Zacaranda (DP). These worlds are in thousand-year orbits (Krokinole, in the middle of the pack, takes 1,642 Earth-years to complete one circle around Rigel). As such, these worlds do not have "seasons" in the usual sense.

In addition to the Concourse are six innermost planets, forming the incandescent Inner Belt, while the Blue Companion orbits one fortieth of a light year out from Rigel.

The seeming implausibility of the habitable worlds existing around such a relatively young star (and populated by presumably autochthonous creatures of such complexity as to suggest the passage of evolutionary time greater than Rigel's lifetime) has led to various theories of large scale terraforming by an unknown alien race (perhaps the Hexadelts) in distant times (KM 3).

For further notes on the Rigel Concourse, see "Appendix V: Concerning the Rigel Concourse."

RIKER'S PLANET a Commonwealth world with gray and red plesiosaurs (SJA).

RLARU a planet in Cetus (SO 1; 7).

ROBERT PALMER'S STAR a brilliant white star in the Cornu section of Ophiuchus, it has 12 planets but only Camberwell is inhabited by humans (NL 1.1).

ROBUNDUS a red star orbited by Glory (DSB).

RODION a famous planet for tourists, far beyond the Wonder Worlds from Halma (E 4).

ROSALIA a world of the Gaean Reach (ArS 1.4).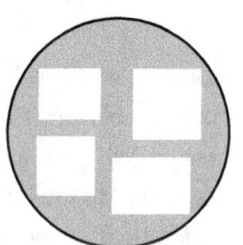
DIAMETER: 7,600 miles.
HYDROGRAPHY: Low (37%).
LAND AREA: 2x Earth.
GEOGRAPHY: Eight large continents (Ottilie, Eclin, Koukou, Yellow Nelly, La Mar, Trinky, Hortense, and Almyra).
FAUNA: Tree-waifs (in the forest canopies), water-waifs (in rivers, swamps, and wet barrens), wind-waifs (in deserts).
POPULATION: Sparse. Port Mona, the largest town, varies from 20,000 to 40,000.

GOVERNMENT: "Double." The Factor's Association governs the ranchers; the Board of Civil Regulations governs the rest. Neither service recognizes the jurisdiction of the other, each claiming paramount authority (Th 5.1).

ROSALINDA an inhabited planet (ST 3).

ROUGE a red giant star, binary to Blanche, orbited by Noir and planet Jexjeka (TOB).

RUBRIMAR CLUSTER ▶ an interstellar nation beyond both the Alastor Cluster and the Gaean Reach (Tr prologue).

RUFOUS PLANET a world of the Alastor Cluster (Tr 14).

S

S-CHA-6 a planet of the Commonwealth era, with caveman autochthons (CG).

SABIK a star with one planet Vadilov, far across the Oikumene from Rigel (KM 2). "Sabik" is an old name for Eta Ophiuchi, 90 l.y. from Old Earth.

SABIK BETAN an alien homeworld of enormous atmospheric pressure (MMU).

SABRIA a wet world of a binary system with Geideon, a dull red giant, and Atreus, a blue green sun (GAB). Fauna include the dekabrach, a seal-like creature with ten arms around its head, which has one central eye; and Stryzkal's Monitor, a non-mobile sea creature with an elastic feeler it uses for food-gathering, spore-disseminating, and exploration.

SADAL SUUD another name for Beta Aquarii, found 550 l.y. from Old Earth.
- *Sadal Suud*—home to the alien mandrakes, with bodies like green-white carrots, having red foliage sprouting from their heads (MMU).

- *Sadal Suud Four*—inhabited world of the Oikumene, with city Vire (F 1).
- *Idora (Sadal Suud XI)*—Oikumene planet notable for having segmented water-worms up to 30 feet in length (KM 6).

SADIRON small moon of Codiron (CHO).

SAFRONILLA a lost world in the far Beyond of the Gaean Reach (NL).

Discovered circa 25,000 by Wilbur Wailey, whose greatest achievement was his "Empire of Song and Glory" in which he stocked this planet with beautiful women tricked, bought, kidnapped, and occasionally contracted (NL 13.5). Wilbur then impregnated each. Fifteen years later he did the same with resulting daughters; later still with granddaughters.

Five thousand years later, it remains undiscovered.

SAGITTA 203 star of Oikumene Beyond (PL 3). See MURCHISON'S STAR.

SAGITTARIUS FFC 32-DE-2930 the Final Functional Catalog term for Gaean Reach planet Ladaque-Royal (NL 11.2).

SAINT WILMIN a wine-exporting world of the Gaean Reach (DTA 5).

SALISBERRY world in the era of contest between Blue Star and Kay (WB).

SANATORIS BETA a star system located 380 l.y. from the Commonwealth planet Fan (SAN).

SANDUSK an Oikumene planet of Fomalhaut (KM 2). Ancient alien ruins, odd human religion, and food that is generally found to taste even worse than it smells.

SANREALE an inhabited world (E 4).

SANSEVERE a Gaean Reach planet with city Lorca and Aetna University (Lu 3.4).

SARBANE a planet of the Gaean Reach (POC 6.0).

SARDANIPOLI presumed Oikumene world, from adjective "Sardanipolitan" (KM 4).

SARKOVY a notorious planet of the Oikumene (DP).Phi Ophiuchi I; Ophiuchus Sector; 210 l.y. from Old Earth.

DIAMETER: 9,600 miles.

SIDEREAL DAY: 37. 2 hours

MASS: 1.40 earths.

GRAVITY: .98 g.

AXIAL TILT: 0° (no seasons).

GEOGRAPHY: A dim world of steppes, swamps, black forests, morasses (SK 4). Hopman Steppe, Gorobundur Steppe, the Great Black Steppe, etc.

POPULATION: Largely nomadic. The settled Sarkoy live in tall wooden houses behind timber palisades, but not even the largest of the towns is secure from attack by bandits and nomads. A Sarkoy hetman is marked with a facial tattoo, a small Maltese cross on his right cheek.

SOCIETY: Famous for the venefices, trained poisoners (PL 1), the Sarkoy are held in low esteem by all other folk of the Oikumene due to their repugnant eating habits as well as their disgusting and exhibitionistic sexual conduct (SK 4).

LAW: "Cooperation" is the term for public execution by poison. A random selection of four capital crimes at a single cooperation:

1. Betrayal of the guild of poisoners.
2. A sexual offense.
3. Throwing sour milk upon his grandmother.
4. Dishonoring a fetish.

RELIGION: A pantheon ruled by Godogma, God of Destiny, who carries a flower and a flail and walks on wheels; tall poles with wheels on high are erected in his honor.

SPORT: "Harbite," the baiting of a harikap, a large bristle-furred semi-intelligent biped of the northern forests. The wretched creatures are first brought into a state of tension through hunger, then thrust into a circle of men armed with pitchforks and torches.

EXPORTS: Poisons, mercenaries.

CURRENCY: SVU.

USEFUL TERMS:

Activant—word for poison.

Alpha—a type of activant that kills within three seconds.

Beta—a type of activant that kills quickly.

Black-tox—a type of activant.

Cluthe—a type of slow-acting activant.

Khet—an epithet, being the name for an obscenely fecund Sarkovy mink.

Meratis—a type of activant.

Patziglog—a type of activant.

Pyrong—a type of activant.

Scop—an honorific, as in "My apologies, Scop Suthiro."

Vole—a type of activant.

SASANI a world of the Oikumene's near Beyond (DP). Aquila GB 1201 IV; Aquila Sector.

SIDEREAL DAY: 21 hours (KM 8).

At some time in the distant past an intelligent race had populated the two north continents, leaving behind the ruins of monumental castles and keeps. In Oikumene times, the world is known mainly for Interchange—a cluster of buildings at the base of a rocky hillock in the Da'ar-Rizm desert. Here the kidnapped are ransomed—see INTERCHANGE for details.

Cities Sagabad, Sul Arsam; starport Nichae (KM 8).

CURRENCY: SVU.

SASSETTA star of Durdane (An 2).

SCHEAT star of planet Badau, located in the Pegasus constellation (FGB 5). "Scheat" is an earlier name for Beta Pegasi, found 196 l.y. from Old Earth.

SCHIAFARILLA CLUSTER see SKIAFFARILLA CLUSTER.

SCLEROTTO PLANET a world located just outside the Commonwealth's border, it orbits two suns, one red, and one blue (UM).

SCROPUS a prison world of the Gaean Reach, fourth planet of Tacton's Star (POC 4.2).

DIAMETER: 6,000 miles.

CORE: Dense.

GRAVITY: Standard (POC 4.3).

SATELLITES: Moon Olanthus shines a silver-green.

GEOGRAPHY: One large continent at north pole, another at south pole, both marked by swirling storms. Ayra, the third continent, is shaped like a salamander and sprawled across the world immediately north of the equator.

HISTORY: Thousands of years previously the world had been lost in the far Beyond. Imbald, the so-called Sultan of Space, had ordered a stately palace of excess to be built—Fanchen Lalu (POC 4.3). In later centuries it passed from hand to hand before becoming a penal institution (the Refectory), an Institute of Advanced Penology, and a laboratory for psychopathological research. At the prison the inmates wear caps upon their heads with color related to each individual's crime.

PRISON CAPS

Color	Criminal
White	Murderers.
Black	Forgers, swindlers, and counterfeiters.
Green	Larcenists.
Orange	Blackmailers.
Purple	Arsonists.
Pink	Mutilators.
Brown	Sexual activists.
Gray	Song stylists.

SEA PLANET inhabited world (NeP).

SECTORS these regions of space seem to be mainly constellations, but there is one "super constellation" (Argo Navis) and one possible portion of a constellation (Cornu). This handbook has used constellations as sectors on occasion (e.g. Lyra Sector for Vega). The source text: ARGO NAVIS, Aquarius (PL 9), AQUILLA, ARIES SECTOR, Auriga (F 14), CORNU SECTOR, ERDIC SECTOR, Nova Celeste (DTA 1), Ophiuchus (PL 10), PERGOLA REGION, Scorpio (KM 5), and Virgo (BD 2).

SEIS one of Nion's 19 moons.

SERAFIM a town on a planet in the Beyond of the Gaean Reach (Lu 3.4).

SHAMIZADE a constellation visible from Zeck in the Alastor Cluster (W 2).

SHAN a pale blue moon of Nion.

SHANITRA the moon of Methel, named after a grotesque clown in the Methlen comic opera (F 12).

SHAUL an orange-colored world orbiting Almach, it has many volcanoes and dust storms (FGB 1). The Shaul are mutated humans having a flesh cowl as protection against their hostile environment. One of the five Langtry races, the others being the Badau, the Eagles, the Kotons, and the Loristanese.

SHAULA Lambda Scorpii (MMU). Alien inhabited system, with autochthons that look like inverted tubs, mottled brown and gray, shiny, with a hundred little sucker-legs underneath, while above an eye in the center like a peri-scope. "Shaula" is a real name for this star, located 700 l.y. from Old Earth.

SHIMWARD GULF a great rift separating the Perseid Arm of the Milky Way Galaxy from the stars of Pegasus and Cassiopeia (Th 4.2). Also known as the Great Lonesome Gulf.

SIBOL the homeworld of the Dirdir (CC 3).

SIGIL the moon of Aume, thus perhaps an earlier name (or alias) for Damar of planet Halma (E); also the name for one of Nion's 19 moons.

SIGMA SCULPTORIS star of Odfars (TLJ). Located 227 l.y. from Old Earth.

SIGRE a planet or star of the Alastor Cluster (Tr 7).

SING a red giant star, binary with Lorca, located in the Purple Rose System (ArS 1.0).

SIRENE a planet of the Oikumene (MM). World of star Mireille.

GEOGRAPHY: Titanic Ocean; cities Fan (spaceport) and Zundar the Forbidden City (a waterway city with docks rather than streets).

POPULATION:

- *Human upper class:* Houseboat owners.
- *Human middle class:* Artisans, free citizens, and laborers.
- *Human lower class:* Slaves.
- *Autochthons:* Night-men, the cannibals that roam the shore.

TECHNOLOGY: Relatively low. There are no aircars, for example. The houseboats are propelled by drayfish.

CURRENCY: UMI used among offworlders.

SOCIETY: All people wear masks all the time and use various musical instruments to accompany spoken communication. The musical instruments have very specialized meanings with regard to rank and situation. Sirenese culture is obsessed with "strakh," a personal social net-worth made up of prestige, honor, face, etc. Strakh determines what masks one can wear. Strakh can be increased by dueling or succeeding at unusual feats; strakh can be decreased by social fumbling—playing the wrong instrument, for example.

A person will wear a different mask according to his own mood, but the strakh levels will always be equal to or lower than his level. A person's mask collection will reveal something of his personality. Here are five examples of offworlders living in Fan:

1. A man with several years of experience, this one chooses a low profile: Tarn Bird, Sophist Abstraction, and Black Intricate.
2. A man with 15 years of experience, he has earned the medium high prestige to wear the Kan Dachan Cycle.
3. An anthropologist who has written books on the culture, he wears the high prestige masks Cave Owl, Star Wanderer, Quincunx,

Wise Arbiter, and Ideal of Perfection, yet his highest is the Equatorial Serpent. He visits Zundar from time to time.

4. A man with over ten years of experience, he wears Emerald Mountain, Triple Phoenix, Prince Intrepid, and Shark God.

5. A man with only five years of experience, but high musicianship, wears the Exo Cambian Cycle (set), and the Nether Denizens (set).

MASKS (A NON-EXHAUSTIVE LIST): Alk Islander, Black Intricate, Bright Sky Bird, Cave Owl, Dragon Tamer, Emerald Mountain, Equatorial Serpent, Exo Cambian Cycle (set), Fire Snake (a dueling type), Forest Goblin, Green Bird, Ideal of Perfection, the Kan Dachan Cycle (Chalekun, Gay Companion, Prince Intrepid, Seavain, and South Wind), Magic Hornet, Moon Moth (minimal strakh), Nether Denizens (set), Pirate Captain, Quincunx, Red Bird, Red Demiurge, Sand Tiger, Sea-Dragon Conqueror (heroic strakh, worn only by princes, heroes, master craftsmen, and great musicians), Shark God, Sophist Abstraction, Star Wanderer, Sun Sprite, Tarn Bird (minimal strakh), Tavern Bravo, Thunder Goblin (a dueling type), Triple Phoenix, Universal Expert, Waldemar, and Wise Arbiter. Slaves wear loose masks of black cloth.

MUSICAL INSTRUMENTS (A NON-EXHAUSTIVE LIST): crebarin (water lute), ganga (hand-sized zither), gomapard (electric oboe), hymerkin (percussive instrument of wood and stone), kiv, krodatch (small stringed soundbox), slubo, skaranyi (a hand-sized bagpipes), stimic (hand-sized bagpipe/trombone), strapan (soundbox with bells), and zachinko (hand-sized concertina). Slaves sing unaccompanied.

SIRENESE MODES OF BEHAVIOR BY MUSICAL INSTRUMENT	
Mode	*Instrument(s)*
Ceremonial	Double-kamanthil, gomapard
Formal	Zachinko
Casual polite	Kiv
Cool withdrawal/disapproval	Stimic
Quiet formality or insult, used upon social inferiors	Krodatch
Intimate or addressing one slightly inferior	Ganga
Talking down to social inferiors	Strapan
Invitation to combat	Hand-bugle
Prelude to combat	Dueling gong (rung once)
Talk to slaves	Hymerkin

Avan esx trobu—to summon a female slave.

Fascu etz Rex ae Toby—summons to slaves Rex and Toby.

SIRIUS a bright star in Canis Major Sector, it is located 8.4 l.y. from Old Earth.

- *Sirius Planet*—world of the byzantaurs, intelligent authochthons with four arms, four legs, and three sexes (SO 5).
- *Sirius Five*—an alien homeworld where the autochthons are torpedo-like amphibians (UM). They export exceptional artichokes (SSS).

SIRNESTE CLUSTER a group of around 200 stars in the Beyond of the Aquarius sector (PL 9). This seems to be the center of the territory accorded to the Demon Prince Viole Falushe in the year 1500. Planets of the cluster include Sogdian and the hidden world hosting the Palace of Love. (M73 is the only known open cluster in Aquarius.)

SISTER PLANETS a group name for Wittenmond, Gietersmond, and Skalkemond (FT 6).

SKALKEMOND a Gaean Reach world, being one of the three Sister Planets of Jinkens Star (FT 6). A financial and educational center. The people who live here are known as Skalks, and they are interested in abstractions.

SKENE star of Aerlith (DM 1). Or Skene, a nation of Big Planet (BP 3).

SKIAFFARILLA CLUSTER a star group between Durdane and Old Earth, it is the most notable object in Durdane's night sky (An 3).

SKYL Lekthwa's star, up and left of Spica from Old Earth (GI 6). This suggests it is within the constellation Virgo.

SKYLARK Eridanus BG12-IV, a prison world (SO 9).

SMADE'S PLANET a world of the middle Beyond (SK 1). The single companion of Smade's Star, an undistinguished white dwarf in a relatively empty region of space. The world is Earth-like.

HISTORY: Smade arrived at this small stony world in 1479 and built Smade's Tavern with the help of ten indentured artisans and ten slaves. This settlement is located precisely on the equator, on a long narrow heath between the Smade Mountains to the south and Smade Ocean to the north. Smade controls about three acres contained within the bounds of a whitewashed stone fence. In the year 1500, the five demon princes met at Smade's Tavern and divided the Beyond among themselves. By 1523, Smade had three wives and eleven children, among them a daughter named Araminta.

FLORA: Lichen, moss, primitive vines and palodendron, pelagic algae which colors the sea black.

FAUNA: White worms in the seabeds, gelatinous creatures in the algae.

SOGDIAN a planet located in the Sirneste Cluster of Aquarius Sector in the Beyond, it is the fifth world of Miel (PL 9).

SIDEREAL DAY: 29 hours.

Comparable to Old Earth in size and atmosphere, it has an hourglass continent, at the south of which is city Atar. The people of Atar are dark-skinned folk with hair dyed orange, wearing white pantaloons and wide complicated turbans (PL 10).

SOMEWHERE a planet of the Rigel Concourse (SK 4).

SOTERAN an alien homeworld with an atmosphere of fluorine, where the autochthons have great filmy wings (MMU).

SOUM a planet of Vergaz, a pink-white star of the Gaean Reach (ArS 7). Soum is a geologically old world, featuring nubbin mountains, innumerable small rivers, and seven mild seas. Soumjiana is the spaceport.

CURRENCY: Sol.

SPADE-ACE the main world of Thieves' Cluster (FGB 4).

SPANGARD a Gaean Reach planet (Lu 8.2).

SPICA star in Virgo Sector, 260 l.y. from Old Earth.
- *Spica VI*—an Oikumene planet, a transit hub with Virgo Junction (BD 2).
- *Spica X*—"Peasant" andromorph homeworld (LC 2).

STAFF a world where human "imagists" engage in six-way contests with each other, projecting images from their minds through machines to public viewscreens at the Imagicon (NeP).

STANISLAS an Oikumene planet, source of the settlers of Methel (F 12).

STAR HOME a small, dense world of the Gaean Reach (POC). Second planet of white dwarf Mireille, with a breathable atmosphere, a congenial climate, and a surface gravity close to Earth's.

SIDEREAL DAY: 20 hours, 23 minutes.

SATELLITES: One moon (Lu 7.1).

GEOGRAPHY: Two continents, the smaller to the north with stone and ice, the larger having steppes, a few ranges of ancient hills, and a minor upthrust of mountains in the far south (Lu 6.5).

SOCIETY:
- *The Ritters*—a patrician caste of uncompromising nomads wandering the seaside littoral.
- *Lallankars*—Ritters who are bandits.

ART: Rugs. "Schmeer" is the adhesive that binds their rugs.

FAUNA:
- *Mereng*—a six-legged predator that lives hidden in narrow tunnels under the grass. Long fanged snout. Body length up to 12 feet.
- *Wump*—a six-legged gigantic herbivore. Forty or fifty feet long, 20 feet high, with a sinuous snout which brings grass to the maw. Ritters domesticate wumps and build trimbles, small residences, upon their broad backs.

STARHOLME an inhabited world (GAB); an inhabited world on the route from Old Earth to Iszm (HI 1). See "Appendix XI: Linkages Between Texts."

STARLEN a world practicing slavery during the Tellurian Empire period prior to the Commonwealth (WT 3).

STARPORT a major city of the Commonwealth, it is probably located on New Acquitain (KT), but *An Encyclopedia of Jack Vance* finds clues it is on Methedeon (KW) or Azul (TOB) as well. Travel from Starport to Moritaba lasts six days (KT). Since 42.5 times 6 equals 255, Starport would seem to be 255 l.y. from Pi Aquarii. (For travel times see "Appendix I: Spaceships.")

STATOR a constellation seen from Zeck (W 2). It is located above the Turtle.

STRYLVANIA probably a city, since it is mentioned in comparison to Stokholm (SK 9).

SULWEN'S PLANET the only planet of Sulwen's Star, located 1,204 l.y. from Old Earth (SUP).

ATMOSPHERE: Frigid nitrogen.

On this world are the enigmatic remains of an ancient battle between two alien starfaring races. The battleground has seven wrecked spaceships. Five have corpses of four-armed humanoids, dubbed "Sea Cows" by the human scientists. The other two wrecks, "Big Blue" and "Big Purple," contain humanoid corpses termed "Wasps." The battle happened 62,000 years before humans discovered the planet. It appears that Big Blue had lifted up and plunged nose first into the ground, where it threatens to topple. Big Purple, with a mortal gash, never left the ground.

SUSSEA a Gaean Reach planet, with city Glame, in a system between Welters and Fluter (Lu 9.7).

SWANNICK'S STAR an orange dwarf star in Taurus sector, orbited by a human colonized planet with a feudalistic society (SO 10).

SYLVANUS a planet of the Gaean Reach, in Virgo sector (EOE 9.2). It is known for its Bang-bird Festival.

SYRENE yellow-white star, trinary with Lorca and Sing, in the Purple Rose System (ArS 1.1).

SYSTEM 🏳 an interstellar nation, centered on Old Earth, which has Channel Planet and Firsk (POT). Also called "Earth System."

T

TACTON'S STAR sun of Scropus, in Pergola Region of the Gaean Reach (POC 4.2).

TAMAR a populous planet in the Nova Celeste sector of the Gaean Reach (DTA 1); or Capella Nine, an inhabited world in the Auriga sector of the Gaean Reach (ArS 1.4).

TANAQUIL city on Bethune (BD 17).

TANQUIL world of the Gaean Reach (GPr 2).

TANTAMOUNT a highly industrialized world of the Rigel Concourse known for its large shipyards (SK 4; 5).

TARTUSZ a constellation seen from Tschai (D 1).

TASSADERO a planet of Zonk's Star in the Gaean Reach (CAD).
POPULATION:
- Zubenites (governed by the Monomantic seminary at Pogan's Point) of Lutwiler Country (100,000).
- Nomads (claiming decent from space pirates) of the steppes (50,000).

- Fexels (ordinary Gaean stock) of Fexel Country, including Fexelburg (3 million total).

TOURISM: Tourists come every year searching for the treasure-laden tomb of Zab Zonk, pirate king of ancient times. The so-called Rivers of Purple Ooze are in reality massive colonies of stinking purple jellyfish that slide across the Great Steppes in columns 400 yards long and 30 yards wide (ArS 7.5).

CURRENCY: Sol.

TAU DRACONIS star, 146 l.y. from Old Earth (MMU). Its planet is TIX.

TAU GEMINI star, 320 l.y. from Old Earth (SK 3). Properly Tau Geminorum. For its Oikumene planet, see VALHALLA.

TAUBRY a planet of the Gaean Reach, it orbits star Vianjeli (POC 2.3).

GEOGRAPHY: Three continents. Liro, the developed one, has 13 cantons (POC 3.1); Farst and Wints are accessible only by special expeditions.

FLORA: The famous cloud-trees.

LAW: Extreme anti-litter laws. "Trivial misdeeds incur confinement in one of the cages at the eastern end of the plaza, for one-half day, one day, or longer."

TOURIST INFO: Houses of public entertainment Categories I, II, and III.

HOUSES OF PUBLIC ENTERTAINMENT	
Category I	Children and sensitive girls may foregather without fear of embarrassment.
Category II	Mature men and women may indulge in serious conversation, and often will exchange jocularities.
Category III	The atmosphere is sometimes a trifle loose. Working spacemen are at ease. The ale is of good quality and ladies are generally less offended by frank and cordial conversation. There is general tolerance of universalities.

TAURUS 61 the star of planet Monago (HI 6). This is likely a reference to 61 Tauri, also known as Delta-1 Tauri, located 153 l.y. from Old Earth.

TEEHALT'S PLANET a beautiful world in the Oikumene's far Beyond, discovered by Lugo Teehalt (SK 11). It is the third world orbiting a golden-white star, the innermost world being an orange cinder and the middle one being a gloomy dismal world.

SIDEREAL DAY: 48 hours long.

FAUNA: The dryads, bipedal trees; subterranean grubs; aerial wasps. There is a curious reproductive relation between the dryads, the grubs, and the wasps (SK 1).

TELLURIAN EMPIRE ⚑ an Earth-centered space empire that was precursor to the Commonwealth, the extent of Tellurian space appears to be about 25 l.y. around Earth (WT 1). At that time Earth's macropolis was Tran (WT 3). While the text in question mentions Hycithil and Starlen, as well as Fan, it is not known whether these are within the Tellurian sphere or outside of it. Other planets include Gavnad, Lojuk, and one at McVann's Star. Two common space routes mentioned are "Earth-Rasalhague" and "Delta Aquila-Sabik" (PBD); Rasalhague (Alpha Ophiuchi) is 47 l.y. from Old Earth and Sabik (Eta Ophiuchi) is 84 l.y. from Old Earth. Another is the "Scorpio-Sagittarius frontier run." An internal area is the Phenesian Blackness, a starless region (PBD). Tellurian rivals include the Clantlalan (WT, PBD) and the Phalid (PF). Far beyond lie Laoome's world and Narfilhet.

TERCE a Gaean Reach world, third planet of orange star Bran (POC 4.4; 5.1).

GEOGRAPHY: Moderate size with a single continent straggling most of the way around the world. There is a great swamp along the west coast, inhabited by ferocious beasts both large and small; elsewhere the fauna is limited to a few leather-winged birds, lizards, fish, and armored insects.

- *Spaceport city*—Dulcie Diver (POC 4.4).
- *Sholo*—a village west of Dulcie Diver, huddled at the base of a scarp rearing a half-mile above the steppe (POC 5.2). Presumably the capital of the Shuja.

- *Mel*—a village on the scarp above Sholo (POC 5.3). Likely the capital of the Meluli.

POPULATION: A sparse human population inhabits six isolated areas, and after 8,000 years the original folk have evolved into five races (POC 5.1).

- *Uche*—stone-age savages of southern mountains, avid cannibals.
- *Shuja*—dwelling on the steppe near the spaceport at the center of the continent. Pale, the color of sallow ivory, with light brown hair. They hunt Meluli for their skins.
- *Meluli*—inhabiting a high plateau at the center of the continent, near the spaceport. Thin and angular with faces the color of clay, they hunt Shuja for their skins.
- *Tarc*—sea folk of the islands off the east coast.
- *Tzingal*—race of the shore.

ART: Human skins are arranged into haunting portrait-like constructions, many sold off-world.

FAUNA: Squonk—a sort of hairless white rat (POC 5.3). For understandable reasons, its name is also a term of insult applied to people.

TERENCE DOWLING'S WORLD an inhabited world far across the Gaean Reach from Cadwal (Th 8.2).

TERRANOVA planet of the Oikumene, Denebola V (BD 3).

TERRESTRIAL EMPIRE ⚑ an interstellar nation centered on Old Earth (AC).

TERTULLIAN a world of the Oikumene which has serfdom (SK 6).

TETHANOR the north star of Koryphon, it forms the Toe of the Basilisk (GPr 8).

TEX WYNDHAM'S PLANET a world of the Gaean Reach notable for possessing distinctive indigenous short-tailed lizards (Th 4.2).

THADDEUS XII a world of the Commonwealth (SSS). Near Chandaria, it is home to the non-human Banshoos.

THALURI SECOND an alien homeworld lacking an atmosphere, but still possessing "plants," "cows," and humanoids (TOB).

THAMBER a lost world of a G8 star (DP). Located somewhere in the Beyond.

> *"Set a course from the old Dog Star*
> *A point to the north of Achernar*
> *Fare until, on the starboard beam,*
> *Six red suns toward a blue sun stream.*
> *Sleight your ship to where afar*
> *A cluster hangs like a scimitar.*
> *Under the hilt to the verge extreme*
> *And dead ahead shines Thamber's gleam"* (KM 9).

GRAVITY: .86 g.

GEOGRAPHY: An Earth-like world with various continents, subcontinents, peninsulas, and a great archipelago of tropical islands. On the west coast of Despaz (the smallest continent) is the principality of Gentilly (capital city Draszane); to the east of Gentilly is Vadrus (city Carrai) and to the south the Land of Misk (Aglabat, the city behind a wall of dark brown stone). Other colorful nations and peoples of Thamber include: Birzul, where the Godmus keeps a harem of 10,000 concubines; Calastang, where the Divine Eye is carried on a vermilion altar 40 yards long and 40 yards high; and the Tadousko-Oi, the fiercest warriors of Thamber, who build their villages on the highest crags and steepest cliffs.

TECHNOLOGY: Medieval by isolation. Castles, knights, romantic deeds, and nearly constant skirmishing.

HISTORY OF THAMBER	
Year	*Event*
500	Thamber colonized (KM 9).
1325	The Time of Great Heroes (KM 6-10).
1525	Oikumene recontact (presumed).

THESSE a world of the Gaean Reach, with city Cassander (FT 1).

TERMS: *"Xtl"* [KSTULL] is the polite honorific in use in Cassander, ultimately derived from the word "stletto" or pirate captain (FT 2).

THETA PISCIUM alien inhabited system (MMU). The aliens in question look like 40 starfish strung on a seven-foot length of bamboo, capable of rolling, walking upright, and jumping. Theta Piscium is located 159 l.y. from Old Earth.

THIEVES' CLUSTER a set of eight stars in the Perseian Limbo, a haven for lost men of all worlds (FGB 4).

THOMBOL an inhabited planet trading with Beland and Mangtse (ST 4).

THUBAN "Thuban" is another name for Alpha Draconis, located 300 l.y. from Old Earth.
- *Thuban Nine*—an inhabited world (ST 3).
- *Thuban XIV*—world with mining operations (MD). Currency: Munit.

THUMBNAIL GULCH a hidden planet in the Beyond (SK 9).
   DIAMETER: 27,900 miles.
   ATMOSPHERE: Not breathable.
   GRAVITY: Tolerable.
   GEOGRAPHY: Many active volcanoes.
This world is actually a dead star that has accumulated such a mantle of light material as to become bigger than its red dwarf companion. It is tide-locked to its dim primary, which fills an eighth of the sky.

TINCTALA a world of the Terrestrial Empire (AC).

TIX Tau Draconis (MMU). Alien inhabited system. The autochthons here are humanoids nine feet tall, spindly, with big heads and no chins. With a skin the color of cockroaches, they have faceted eyes and sucker-tipped fingers. "TIX" is not a real name, but Tau Draconis is found 146 l.y. from Old Earth.

TOE OF THE BASILISK a constellation, or a detail of a constellation, seen from Koryphon (GP 8).

TRAN a Gaean Reach planet, transportation hub between Fluter and Morlock (Lu 6.2). Main city: Port Pallas.

TRANQUE a world of the Gaean Reach, also known as Bellatrix V, which see (EOE 5.2). Also a Float on Blue World (BW 1).

TRASNOY a planet of the Gaean Reach (NL 13.4).

TRIPTOLEMUS an inhabited world considered by some to be the home world of mankind (E 4). Named after a demigod of farming in Greek mythology.

TRISKELION a world of the Alastor Cluster, the source of settlers of Rhamnotis (Tr 3).

TRULLION: ALASTOR 2262 a watery world of the cluster (Tr). The lone planet of a small white star.

GEOGRAPHY: A small world, mostly water, with a single narrow continent, "Merlank," at the equator (named for the lizard it resembles). The mountains have opals and emeralds.

SOCIETY: Aristocracy at top, nomad Trevanyi at bottom (Tr 6). The athletic sport game hussade (see "Appendix II: Sports"), played throughout the Alastor Cluster, is something of a planetwide passion.

TRILL COSTUME: The "paray," an easy skirt-like garment worn by both men and women.

TRILL LIFESTYLE: Trills work perhaps an hour each day, occasionally as much as two or three. Leisure activities include musing from the verandah of their ramshackle houses, and "star-watchings," informal parties. "Going off to visit friends" is a Trill euphemism for *cauch*-crazy lovers going off to camp in the wilds.

TRILL COUNTER-PHILOSOPHY: Fanscherade. Begun by Junius Farfan of Trullion, the Fanschers feel that each person must establish exalted goals and fulfill them if he can. They have shorn hair and wear odd gray clothes with small medallions on their left shoulders, the women in austere gray gowns of durable white duck.

TREVANYI: The exactness and intensity of the Trevanyi is a sharp contrast to the imprecision of the Trill. They are a nomadic folk of a distinctive racial stock, prone to thievery, sorcery, and other petty chicaneries. An excitable, passionate, vengeful people, they consider *cauch* a poison and guard the chastity of their women with fanatic zeal. Trevanyi wagons are ponderous boats with wheels, capable on either land or water.

TREVANYI COSTUME (MALE): Black breeches tucked into sagging black boots, a loose shirt of beige silk, a colored neckerchief, and a flat black hat.

TREVANYI RELIGION: A black bird carries their ghosts to the Vale of Xian, where they wander in peace. But folk eaten by merlings leave no ghosts.

The Vale of Xian, known by the Trills as the Vale of Green Ghosts, is located near the mountain town Circanie. Here Trevanyi bury lesser dead among the trees—the true and sacred vale is further in.

Urmank the Ghost-killer seems to be a lightning god of the Trevanyi.

AUTOCHTHONS: Amphibious half-intelligent merlings, they hunt humans and vice versa.

FAUNA:

- *Cavout*—a grazing food animal.
- *Curest*—edible crab-like sea insect.
- *Karpoun*—a feral tiger-like beast.
- *Mudworm*—edible.
- *Quorl*—a type of edible mollusk living in beach sand.
- *Tanchinaro*—a black and silver fish of the Far South Ocean.

GOVERNMENT: Rudimentary, handled mainly by a small middle caste of officials. There are twenty prefectures, the most detailed of which is Jolany Prefecture, located east of Straveny Prefecture on the southern coast. Prefectures Minch and Gulkin neighbor Jolany Prefecture, one presumably inland to the north and the other further east along the coast.

Port Maheul, with one of only four spacefields on the planet, is the largest town of Straveny Prefecture.

The market town Welgen, located one hundred miles east of Port Maheul, is the largest settlement in Jolany Prefecture. It is notable for having a hussade stadium and a *prutanshyr*. The Fens begin east of Welgen.

LAW: "Prutanshyr" is the macabre ritual of gelding and public execution by suspension from hooks in a glass cauldron of boiling oil, all to the accompaniment of sad, sweet music.

INTERSTELLAR TRADE: Unimportant—only four spaceports (Port Gaw in the west, Port Kerubian on the north coast, Port Maheul on the south coast, and Vayamenda in the east). "Cauch," an aphrodisiac drug derived from the spore of a mountain mold, is by far the most valuable commodity produced on Trullion.

CURRENCY: Ozol.

USEFUL TERMS:

Avness—the pale hour immediately before sunset.

Fanscher—a follower of Fanscherade.

Fanscherade—name of an anti-social yet altruistic creed or movement, from old Glottisch term "Fan," a corybantic celebration of glory.

Forlostweena—Trevanyi jargon for an urgent mood compelling departure.

Lyssum—a named month of Trullion.

Narwoun—a coiled, full-throated musical instrument.

Racq—a powerful distilled beverage.

Spageen—individual in a state of rut ("spag").

Urush—derogatory Trevanyish cant for a Trill (citizen of Trullion).

Varmous—a Trevanyi term for dirty, infamous, scurrilous; often applied to Trills.

TSAMBARA: ALASTOR 1317 a world of the Alastor Cluster (Ma 4).

TSCHAI an ancient world, the amber-trap graveyard of interstellar empires (PA). Solitary planet of a K2 star. Carina 4269 I; Carina Sector; 212 l.y. from Old Earth.

DIAMETER: Somewhat larger than Earth.

SATELLITES: Two small moons, Az (pink) and Braz (blue).

YEAR: 488 days (1.336 Earth years).

GEOGRAPHY: A grey-brown planet with six continents—Charchan (largest), Kotan, Kislovan, Kachan, Rakh, and Vord. The Draschade Ocean (Between Kislovan and Kachan), the Schanisade Ocean (opposite hemisphere from Draschade).

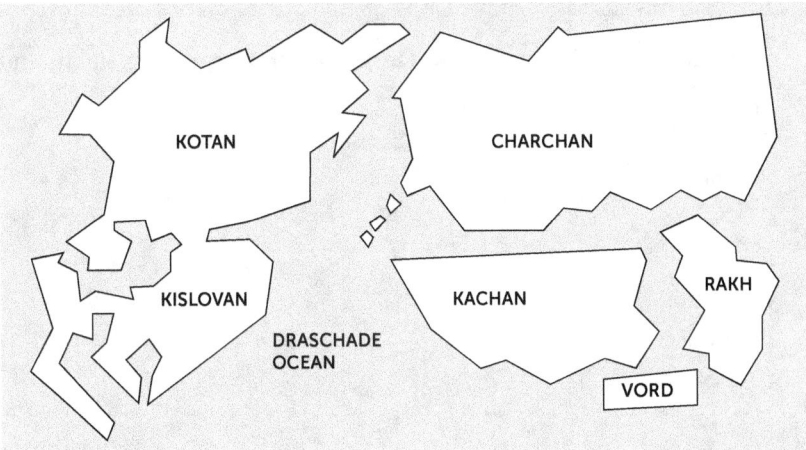

GOVERNMENT: Balkanized into three deadlocked empires, a vestigial empire, and numerous petty kingdoms.

POPULATION:

- *Deadlocked empires:* Blue Chasch (far west of Kotan), Dirdir (Kislovan), Wankh (Kachan). Each group also has an associated race of servitors (Blue Chaschmen, Dirdirmen, Wankhmen), humans bred to be servants. The servitors have been molded and mold themselves to resemble their captors, each holding themselves to be superior to the "submen" unaffiliated with aliens.
- *Vestigial empire:* Old Chasch, now mainly in the Jang Pinnacles of west Kotan. And their servants, the Old Chaschmen.
- *Petty kingdoms:* Human. Cath, the largest and most technologically advanced, is located on the west coast of Charchan.
- *Nomads:* Green Chasch; various independent human groups (Berl Totems, Emblem Men, Ilanths, Kite-Fighters, Mad Axes, Niss, Yellow-Blacks, etc.) of varying levels of technological ability (for example, the Emblem Men are more-or-less medieval yet use electric motorcycles as scout vehicles).
- *Hunter/Gatherers:* Marshmen (stone age humans).
- *Displaced autochthons:* Pnume (with their subterranean city museums and servator Pnumekin).

EXPORTS: None.

CURRENCY: Sequins (planet wide, derived from special plants found only in the Carabas desert of Kislovan).

USEFUL TERMS (TSCHAI UNIVERSAL):

Numbers

1	Aine
2	Sei
3	Dros
4	Enser
5	Nif
6	Hisz
7	Yaga
8	Managa
9	Nuwai
10	Tix

Words

Bevol—an evil spirit, perhaps the Devil.

Clari—name of the constellation where Earth is located.

Harasthy—a demon.

Issir—sword.

Rhadamth—a sea-demon.

Sagorio—a nine-headed god.

Tartusz—name of a constellation.

Tatap—Father.

Vam—Mother.

DAYS OF THE 10-DAY WEEK

Tschai	*English*
Azday	Monday
Ilsday	
Ivensday	

NAMED MONTHS (IN SEQUENCE)

Temas

Meumas

Azaimas

BLUE CHASCH: The Chasch homeworld is Godag. The Blue Chasch have a powerful olfactory sense, akin to that of bloodhounds, and they augment this with technological aids. They love to bargain, but they gladly cheat at every chance. They have an obsession with complication as an end to it-self—a Chasch artifact will have excessive ornamentation.

> BLUE CHASCH SOCIETY: The Blue Chasch have developed a reli-gion for their Chaschmen whereby the servitors are told that if they are virtuous in life, at death they will be reborn as Blue Chasch. The Blue Chasch reinforce this by faking the finding of newborn Blue Chasch within the opened craniums of dead Chaschmen.

DIRDIR: The Dirdir homeworld is Sibol. The Dirdir spirit remains feral, and hunting is a lust for them.

Among the Dirdir there are a dozen styles of male sexual organs, and fourteen of the female. Only certain pairings are possible. "For example, type one male is compatible with only types five and nine female. Type five female adjusts only to type one male, but type nine female has a more gen-eral organ and is compatible with types one, eleven and twelve male" (D 17).

> DIRDIR SOCIETY: The Dirdir are arranged in 28 castes. The Dirdirmen have four castes, from highest to lowest: the Immaculates (who are allowed certain Dirdir privileges, including *zs'hanh* and the hunt), the Intensives, the Estranes, and the Cluts.
>
> USEFUL TERMS (DIRDIR):
>
> *Dr'ssa, dr'ssa, dr'ssa*—a phrase that commands arbitration for wrongs suffered.
>
> *Hs'ai hs'ai, hs'ai*—a phrase that compels help.
>
> *H'so*—marvelous dominance.
>
> *Pn'hanh*—corrosive or metal-bursting sagacity, applicable only to the highest caste.
>
> *Tsau'gsh*—a band of hunters, from a word meaning initiative; prideful endeavor; unique enterprise; lunge toward glory.
>
> *Zhna-di*—individual initiative, a "great dashing leap, trailing light-ning-like sparks."
>
> *Zs'hanh*—the virtue of "contemptuous indifference to the activities of others." This applies to castes four through thirteen.

PNUME SOCIETY: The Pnume are subterranean. The Pnumekin have three genders: males, females, and mother-women. The Pnumekin general food includes some sort of chemical additive that keeps the females in a non-menstrual state, mimicking the reproductive strategy of social insects such as ants.

USEFUL TERMS (PNUME):

Ghaun—surface of Tschai.

Ghian—inhabitant of surface of Tschai.

Gol'eszitra—listening monitor.

Gzhindra—a Pnumekin exiled to the surface.

Zuzhma kastchai—the Pnume word for themselves.

WANKH SOCIETY: The Wankh are the most recent arrival to Tschai. Their language is completely different from the others, and the Wankhmen are the only translators. Through this, the Wankhmen have managed to put themselves in a more superior position to their patrons than any other servant groups.

HUMAN OR "SUBMEN" SOCIETIES—FROM NOMADS TO NATIONS: Two examples to sketch out a tribe of nomads and a nation state.

- NOMADS: EMBLEM MEN OR KRUTHE

  The emblems referred to in their name are unique devices worn by every man on his hat. Onmale is the supreme emblem, and its wearer is tribal leader. Other named emblems are Vaduz and Piluna (notorious for dark deeds).

  Technology: They ride electric motorcycles for scouting, and use boy-lofting kites for spotting, but they use leap horses for their raids against caravans.

  Religion: Magicians of the moons Az and Baz.

  Terms: "Kruthsh'geir" is, roughly, a man who has defied and defiled his emblem, and hence perverted his destiny.

- NATION STATE: CATH

  The society goes through cycles or "rounds" lasting hundreds of years. The current round is orthodox, in contrast to the previous round that had a cult about a human world in the constellation Clari. This cult had its origin among Dirdirmen.

  Ethnicity: The Golden Yao, a very old golden skinned race, said to be a hybrid of the First Tans and First Whites.

  Technology: Air-car taxis, monorail trains, but otherwise there is a 19th century feel.

Society: The previous round ended with the devastation of two cities, Settra and Ballisade, by aerial torpedos. The source of these was unknown, but the Dirdir were suspected. This trauma has given rise to "awaile," a murderous amok state. If a person of Cath is deeply shamed, he or she kills as many people as possible, then becomes apathetic. The murderer is given a terrible public execution, which gives a cathartic experience for the others. The Yao are highly sensitive to shame. Mysterious enemies destroy their cities; while they suspect the Dirdir, they dare no response, and must cope with helpless rage and shame.

HISTORY OF TSCHAI

Years Ago		Event
Tschai	*Earth*	
7 million	9.3 million	Earliest Pnume records; history begins on Tschai around the time of the Shivvan invasion (Pn 12). On Earth, a time of grasslands, savannahs, and megafauna.
? million	? million	Gjee invasion. Fesa invasion. Hsi invasion (Pn 12).
100,000	133,600	Old Chasch arrive on Tschai (CC 4).
90,000	120,000	Blue Chasch arrive on Tschai, war with Old Chasch, Green Chasch introduced as shock troops.
60,000	80,000	Dirdir arrive on Tschai, fight with Chasch to stalemate.
52,400	70,000	Dirdir bring humans (First Tans) to Tschai; escaped humans mutate into Marshmen.
20,000	26,700	Emergence of Steppe humans; Old Chasch enter senescence on Tschai; Dirdir bring First Whites (CC 4).
10,000	13,000	Space war between Dirdir and Wankh spreads to Tschai when Wankh build forts on Rakh and South Kachan.
7,485	10,000	Human history begins on Earth (CC 2).
150	200	Golden Yao (humans) of Cath build interstellar radio, are crushed by the Dirdir (according to the Golden Yao; CC 4) or the devious Wankhmen (servants of the Wankh).

TURTLE a constellation seen from Zeck, "along the edge of the carapace" of which the star Dwan is seen (W 2). It is located below Stator.

TYR GOG Pegasus KE58, the star of Rhea (Th 4.2).

TYRHOON a planet of the Gaean Reach on which there are rumored to be the sunken ruins of an alien civilization (Th 6.2).

UNFORTUNATE WASTE a boundary of the Alastor Cluster (Ma prologue).

UNICORN a planet of the Rigel Concourse in the Oikumene (SK 4); a constellation in the Alastor Cluster (Ma 4); a constellation seen from Vermazen in the Gaean Reach (POC 1.8).

UNICORN GULF a region of the galaxy beyond Earth-dominated space (ST 1). About a thousand light years toward the galactic rim.

URBAN a small, yellow-green star orbited by Glory (DSB).

USHANT a soft, kind world of the Gaean Reach, hospitable to tourists, with a highly civilized population (NL 10.5).

    CAPITAL: Dimplewater, City of the Thousand Bridges.

    CULTURE: The inhabitants are intensely sophisticated and sensitive to all the aesthetic nuances. Their most distinctive trait is extreme autonomy, which prompts them to live alone. This privacy is modified by yacht club activities, scholarly seminars, and camping trips with their children (who are otherwise neglected).

    "Tamsour" is an untranslatable term that means something like "the totality of an individual's life condensed into one burst." At random intervals a person becomes unaccountably overstressed and explodes with a dramatic peroration, a performance that has come to be expected. Tamsour is the theme, and the substance is usually personal aggrandizement, sometimes a hint of self-pity, but never an apology for past deeds. Then follows suicide, as dramatically and poetically as possible. Around one percent of the population will do this.

V

VADILOV an Oikumene world, the sole planet of Eta Ophiuchi (KM 2).

VALE there are two different planets of this name.
1. A world of the Polymark Cluster, known as a place of anarchy and high spontaneity, where their language has few conventions (LP 8).
2. A world of the Oikumene, seventh planet of Virgo 912 (PL 10). There are druids here.

VALHALLA an Oikumene world at Tau Geminorum, Valhalla is the birthplace of the IPCC circa 1075 (SK 3). It is the sixth world of its system (PL 10). Tau Geminorum is found 320 l.y. from Old Earth.

VALISANDE a planet of the Rigel Concourse (SK 4).

VAN KAATHE'S STAR sun of the Oikumene planet Moudervelt (BD 10; 11).

VANELLO resort world of the Oikumene, located at the "back of Scorpio" (KM 5). Its annual "Floration Rite" involves sinuous supports to 45 sepalic platforms. A platform supported by a long flexible stem raises a priestess dressed in flower petals, while another similar platform raises a table supporting a book, a beaker, and a human skull.

VARSILLA a world of the Gaean Reach (DTA 8; 10). It has nine oceans, ten thousand sea peaks, and eleven million islands.

VEGA a star of Lyra Sector, 25 l.y. from Old Earth (DP).

VEGA SYSTEM	
Orbit	*World*
I	Padraic—a scorched cinder.
II	Mona—a hot rockball.
III	Noaille—tidelocked hellish orb of fire and ice.
IV	Cuthbert—inhabited.
V	Aloysius—densely populated.
VI	Boniface—inhabited.

In addition to the planets, there is Killarney, a penal satellite (SK 3).

HISTORY: The First Vegan Wars were Aloysians vs. Ambrosians (F 3). The Aloysians won, and named the place.

VEIDRANU an alien home world at Psi Hercules (MMU). Veidranu is a jungle world with Type B humanoids that are fragile, covered with moth-dust, and have hair of pink, green, and blue film. More properly Psi Herculis is an earlier name for Nu Boötis, which applies to two different stars: one a K-type giant 872 l.y. from Old Earth, the other a binary pair 430 l.y. from Old Earth.

VERGAZ pink-white sun of Soum (ArS 7).

VERLAREN a world of the Oikumene also known as Epsilon Sagittae II, it is the second planet of Komred (F 3). Epsilon Sagittae is 473 l.y. from Old Earth.

VERMAZEN world of star Dianthe in the Gaean Reach (POC 1.1; 2.1). A pleasant, civilized world, located near the Pergola Region. Salou Sain is a major city with a spaceport.

VIANJELI Taubry's star, in the Gaean Reach (POC 2.3).

VINDEMIATRIX alien home world found at Eta Virginis (MMU). Here the autochthons are translucent eels with dorsal spines and four hands around their mouths; their brains are in long spinal bands that phosphoresce visibly during thought. "Vindemiatrix" is a real name for what is properly Epsilon Virginis, located 110 l.y. from Old Earth.

VIRGINIS REEF a region of space marking the limits of Earth System's authority (BP 3).

VIRGO 912 star of the Oikumene planet Vale (PL 10). This might be 91 G. Vir, a Ko star found 339 l.y. from Old Earth.

VIRGO AXX-1 THIRTEEN an inhabited planet of the Gaean Reach (NL 13.11).

VIRGO GGP 922 region of the Gaean Reach where Naharius is located (POC 1.7).

VIRGO JUNCTION a town or city on Spica VI (BD 2). Located in Virgo Sector, Spica is 280 l.y. from Old Earth.

W

WALE a world where slavery is practiced (E 15).

WALPURGIS a world of the Rigel Concourse (SK 4).

WELTERS a Gaean Reach planet in a system near Sussea (Lu 9.7). City: First Camp.

WICKER a planet of the Gaean Reach (FT 8).

WIGG'S WISP a region of the Gaean Reach (NL 7.3).

WIRFIL an Oikumene planet where the Institute opposed the use of pesticides (BD 9).

WITTENMOND in the Gaean Reach, one of the three Sister Planets of Jinkens Star. The inhabitants, called Witts, are traders and merchants, with a highly stratified social status system (FT 4).

WONDER WORLDS a group of marvelous planets in the Mirabilis Cluster where wealthy tourists from Halma sometimes travel (E 4).

WYST: ALASTOR 1716 a utopian world of the cluster (W).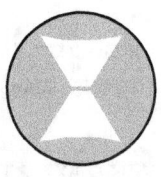
Single planet of Dwan, a white star known as the Eye of the Crystal Eel in Giampara's Realm, low to the side of Alastor Cluster. Wyst is small and dense.

DIAMETER: 5,000 miles.

DENSITY (CALCULATED): 8.7 (where a planet of solid iron = 8)

HISTORY: Colonized for a thousand years, a hundred and seventy five years ago the Great Hemispheric War between Trembal and Tremora destroyed both nations—refugees flowed to the equatorial littoral of Arrabus. One hundred years ago the Egalic revolution swept Arrabus. The agricultural lands of north and south were abandoned and are now the Weirdlands of forest and ruins.

GEOGRAPHY: Opposed continents Trembal and Tremora, together shaped like a thick-waisted hourglass extending 4,000 miles, separated at the equator by the 100-mile wide Salaman Sea. Northern Trembal has the Northern Gulf; Southern Tremora has the Moaning Ocean. On the other side of the planet lie the island continents Zumer and Pombal.

At the equator, Trembal and Tremora both have 20 mile-litorals upon which are founded a few high-density cities. Trembal's are Propunce and Waunisse; Tremora's are Uncibal and Serce. These cities merge and are considered sections of one world city, which is called Arrabus.

Balad is a coastal town on Tremora's Moaning Ocean, separated from Arrabus by nearly two thousand miles of Weirdlands. Balad is a contractor town, being something like a colony with a new-made lord, a powerful contractor who styles himself a "Grand Knight." Along with this feudal government, the denizens have a medieval mindset about witches, the "witches" in this case being mute nomads. Their periodic witch hunts are very much like fox hunts, with hounds. Aside from murdering witches, some Balad men specialize in raping the "kits."

CLIMATE: Damp and cool.

POPULATION:

- *Dominant Colonists:* 3,000,000,000+ urban dwellers in Arrabus (750 million per city).

- *Outland Colonists:* Shunk breeders and riders on Zumer and Pombal.
- *Vital Fringe Colonists:* Contractors, gypsies, farmers of Weirdlands.
- *Displaced Colonists:* Witches.

COMPLEXION: Of mixed ethnicity, they are pale to medium in tone.

ARRABIN GOVERNMENT: Egalitarian utopia. The Whispers, nominal rulers of Wyst, are five people chosen by lot.

ARRABIN TECHNOLOGY: In decline for the last hundred years—many of the factories essential to supporting the megacities are in danger of shutting down due to decrepitude. Yet the manways, sliding pedestrian roadways completed thirty years after the egalic revolution, are still considered one of the Wonders of the Cluster.

Supporting Arrabin technology are the contractors, their technicians and mechanics. To Arrabins they are a caste of interplanetary riffraff, entirely outside egalistic dignity. The Arrabins think of them as servile work masters, eager to oblige the noble egalists and at all times conscious of their inferior status.

ARRABIN CULTURE: The Arrabins typically wear gaily patterned smocks, short trousers, and sandals of synthetic fibers. They wear their hair teased out into extravagant puffs and fringes. They are excited only by food.

ARRABIN SOCIETY: The workweek is 13 hours long. Citizens are randomly assigned low drudge (menial or factory work) or high drudge (management). Competence is considered anti-egalic, or "elitist." The population is housed in large apartment blocks, each twenty-three stories high and built to accommodate 3,000 people, two per small apartment. There is no music, but a wide variety of suicide shops are available. The local version of hussade (a team sport popular throughout the Alastor Cluster) is curiously variant—the sheirl of the losing team is publicly defiled by Claubus, a twelve-foot wooden effigy.

All food is synthetic, based upon a substance called "sturge" (ultimately a closed loop recycling product) which is further processed into three forms: gruff (foodcake), deedle (beverage), and wobbly (dessert). Since local food is so bland, offworlders (even resident aliens) are inevitably pestered for tasty food and drink, and a popular weekend adventure for denizens of Arrabus is "forage," dangerous expeditions into the Weirdlands for the purpose of raiding "bonter" (natural foods) from the farms. Since no intoxicants are produced officially, bootleg brew made from food scraps is ubiquitous.

ARRABIN LAW: There are no police, only "Monitors" who nevertheless fail to investigate even probable homicide. The Uncibal Penal Camp is full of sexivators, shirkers, shiftills, flamboyants, performers, and violeers. Otherwise it is generally known that "snerging (theft) ensures egalism" (W 3).

ARRABIN TAXES: Citizens pay with hormones and glandular extracts, two days each year. Convicted criminals contribute more.

ARRABIN DIALECT: Their language avoids distinction of gender. Masculine and feminine pronouns are replaced by neutral ones. "Parent" replaces both "mother" and "father;" "sibling" stands for "brother" and "sister." When distinctions must be made, colloquialisms are used, almost brutally offensive in literal translation, reference being made to the genital organs.

TRANSPORTATION: Extensive moving beltways in Arrabus are one of the acknowledged Wonders of Alastor Cluster. Omnibuses carry excursionists from the city; aircars are used by contractors for businesses and "elitist" lords of realms beyond the Weirdlands (e.g., the Grand Knight of Balad).

SPACEPORTS: Uncibal has a spaceport. Balad, on the coast of the Moaning Ocean to the far south, has a landing field.

EXPORTS: Human glands are milked of secretions for offworld export.

CURRENCY: Drivet. Salary for drudge. Ten tokens paid for each hour worked. Five hundred tokens equal only about one ozol.

DAYS OF THE WEEK

Wyst	English
Twisday	Tuesday
Fyrday	Friday
Dwanday	Sunday
Aensday	
Onasday	

USEFUL TERMS:

Bad Worlds—non-egalistic planets.

Beatific—the quality of leisurely, luxurious, and well-arranged existence.

Bombah—wealthy offworlder; by extension, a tourist. "Loud Bombah" is an important and powerful off-worlder. "Loudest Bombah" is the Connatic.

Bonter—natural food.

Bumbuster—an omnibus.

Catrape—offensive epithet signifying bedragglement, offensive odor, and vulgarity of manner.

Chwig—a vice, a person overly fond of bonter.

Condaptery—the science of information management, including cybernetics.

Elitist—the opposite of egalic.

Guttrick—any visitor who grumbles over the lack of bonter.

Mutuality—the Arrabin code of conduct, from mutuality of interest.

Non-mutual—criminal.

Sexivation—to emphasize sexual difference. A punishable crime.

Shauk chutt—an oath meaning "damnation and vileness."

Shrick—a pejorative epithet, untranslatable.

Snerge—thief.

Snergery—thievery.

Swill—illegal brew. A heavy beer prepared from salvaged gruff, industrial glucose, and sometimes tar-pods from the roof gardens.

Wump—food.

Wumper—communal food room; refectory.

CRISIS: The infrastructure (factories, housing, etc.) is breaking down faster than egalic (amateur) efforts can repair it.

X

XAMPIAS a planet of the Alastor Cluster (Ma 4).

XANARRE a Gaean Reach world famous for its alien ruins and floating cloud-cities (ArS 1.6)

XANTHENOROS a planet of the Gaean Reach (NL 12.6).

XENCHOY a populated planet (ST 9). Travelers beware: on Xenchoy only a man intending suicide will possess a girl out of wedlock, so she will dutifully try to knife him in the back at his most vulnerable moment.

XI ARIETIS star in Aries, its seventh world is inhabited (SO 12).

XI AURIGAE star of planet Iszm (HI 5), it is an A2 V star located 240 l.y. from Old Earth.

XI PUPPIS X this planet features "Monument Cliff," enigmatic ruins of a forerunner starfaring civilization (KM 3). Xi Puppis is located 1,200 l.y. from Old Earth. See also GHNARUMEN.

XION a world of the Rigel Concourse (SK 4).

Y

YAN Earth-like planet of Hydra GRA 4442, colonized by humans in ancient times (SO 10).

YANAZ one of Dion's 19 moons.

YAPHET a mild world of the Gaean Reach, being the eighth of eleven circling Gilbert's Green Star, inhabited by people "intent on living at their fullest potential" (Th 3.2).

YELLOW ROSE sun of Nilo-May (NL 13.3).

YELLOW SUN PLANET an inhabited world, the source of Lily Milk ceramic ware (BD 4).

YS a planet of the Rigel Concourse originally settled by Reformed Rationalists who, to the scandal of others in the Oikumene, allow sibling marriage (SK 8). Ys seems to be a "warm" world of islands, so it is probably one of the first seven in the Concourse, coming before Alphanor.

Z

ZACARANDA a world of the Rigel Concourse (SK 4). The name might be a corruption of "jacaranda," a type of flower.

ZADE planet Phi Orionis II (SO 7).

ZAEL blue sun of Durdane (An 2).

ZALMYRE a Gaean Reach world, being a tourist planet of Bhutra, along with Eiselbar and Dwet (MT 11).

ZANGWILL REEF a structure of galactic geography, being a "flowing band of stars with a baleful reputation" on the far side of the Great Hole from the Gaean Reach (MT Preface).

ZARJUS an inhabited planet whose vegetation is colored yellow, orange, and lime green (ST 8).

ZECK: ALASTOR 503 a watery world (W). A planet of Mur, an orange star located in Cassadense's Realm of the Alastor Cluster.

GEOGRAPHY: One hundred thousand islands scattered across 100 seas, inlets, and channels.

ARTS: Mooring posts for houseboats are ornate, symbols of status, profession, or special interests (W 2).

CURRENCY: Ozol.

ZONK'S STAR primary of planet Tassadero (ArS 7.4).

ZOÖR the Chasch planet believed by Blue Chaschmen to be the homeworld of humans (CC 11).

ZOSMEI one of the moons of Nion.

ZUMBERWALTS a group of inhabited planets in the Terrestrial Empire (AC).

STAR MAP COLLECTION

There are several different orientations used in galactic cartography. For example, in the case of a top-down view of the galaxy, which is very useful for showing the spiral shape and the galactic core, there are at least three forms. One places the galactic core at the top of the page (the "north"), and another puts it at the right-hand side of the page (the "east"), whereas the scientists prefer the core to be at the bottom of the page (the "south"). Because these forms are mutually exclusive, one must sift a text carefully for clues as to the type being used. (Of course there is the possibility of different forms being used in the same era—in fact, the story "Sabotage on Sulfur Planet" illustrates exactly this problem, at one point contrasting a Cartesian system of x, y, z co-ordinates with the astronomers' system of R.A., declination, and distance.)

At the beginning of *Maske: Thaery* is a particularly clear and unambiguous paragraph on the topic. For starters, it is given that the point of view is not from above the galactic disk, but rather from within the middle of the disk. This makes perfect sense for both the traveler voyaging through space as well as the armchair enthusiast. Here is each part of the instructive paragraph, followed by commentary.

- *"The conventions of galactic direction are like those of a rotating planet. The direction of rotation is east, the opposite west."*

This sounds simple. "Direction of rotation" means a counterclockwise spin viewed from above the north pole—thus east on Earth, because the spin is such. But is the spin of the Milky Way galaxy also counterclockwise viewed from above? It seems to be the opposite, to be spinning in a clockwise direction, which threatens to make galactic east into the left-hand side of the page. Then again, this depends upon whether the orientation is toward the core or toward the rim, since east and west will change sides.

Thus ambiguity creeps into a seemingly simple and straightforward description. The chance of being wrong is fifty percent. To preserve the original tone I will assume that east is the right side of the page when looking toward the galactic core. Thus east is in the direction of the constellation Cygnus, and west is in the direction of the constellation Vela.

- *"When the fingers of the right hand extend in the direction of rotation, the thumb points to the north and the opposite is south."*

The center plane of the galactic disk is the equator of the map. North is the upper half of the galactic disk, and south is the lower half.

- *"'Inward' and 'outward' refer to motion toward or away from the center of the galaxy."*

Inward is toward the galactic core (in the direction of constellation Sagittarius), and outward is toward the rim (in the direction of constellation Auriga).

Taking all this into consideration, I have created a series of two maps, one facing Inward and the other facing Outward. To the east, that is, somewhere between 225° and 315°, are two enigmatic locations. In the time of the Oikumene, Brinktown is located in the "North East Middle Beyond" (SK 1), which would put it in the northern half, somewhere in the upper right quadrant of the Inward map or the upper left quadrant of the Outward map. For the later Gaean Reach, its "eastern fringe" is at the Great Hole, beyond which glitters Zangwill Reef (MT 1).

Since the Alastor Cluster is said to be "out toward the rim" (Tr 1), that would be somewhere on the Outward map.

Inward Map

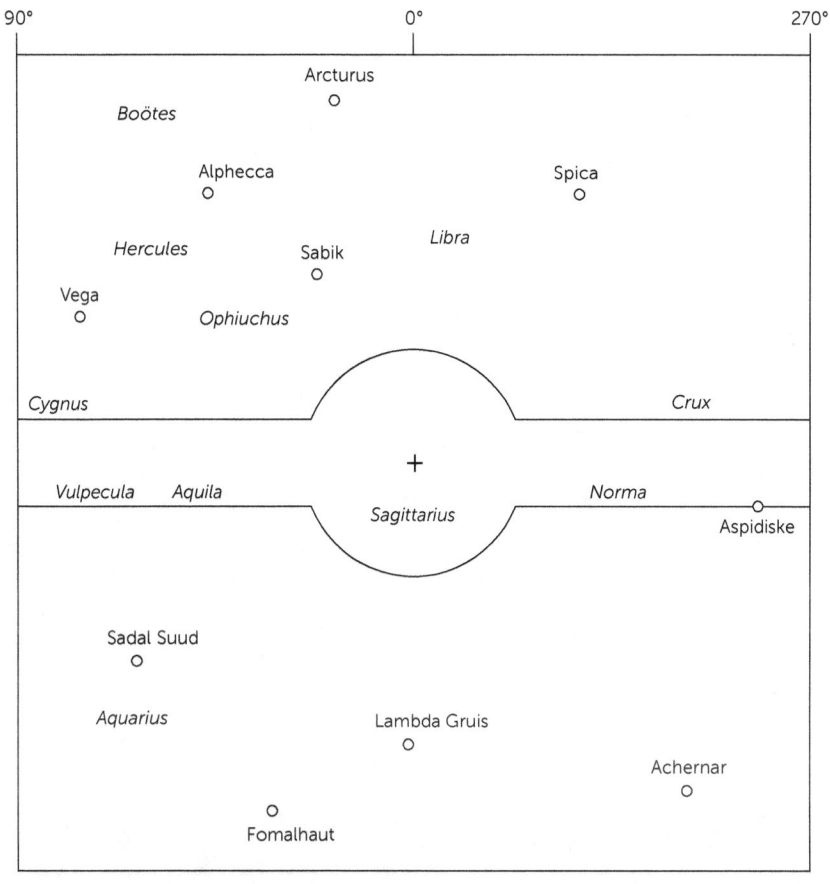

Outward Map

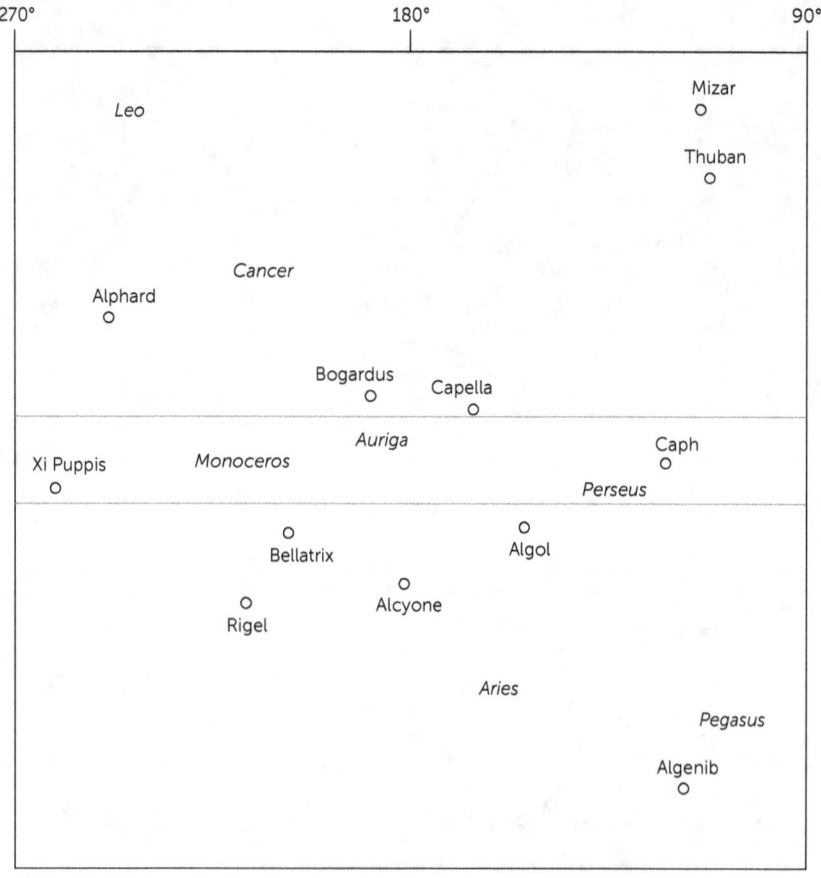

Twelve Sectional Maps

The two square maps are followed by a series of pie-slice maps showing a top-down view for known stars within 1,200 l.y. of Old Earth. Each section map is named after a constellation at the galactic equator, but actually shows stars above and below the disk, as well as within the disk. In clockwise order, like the hours on a clockface, they are:

1. Norma Section
2. Crux Section
3. Vela Section
4. Puppis Section
5. Monoceros Section
6. Auriga Section

7. Perseus Section
8. Casseiopeia Section
9. Cygnus Section
10. Vulpecula Section
11. Aquila Section
12. Sagittarius Section

Norma Section

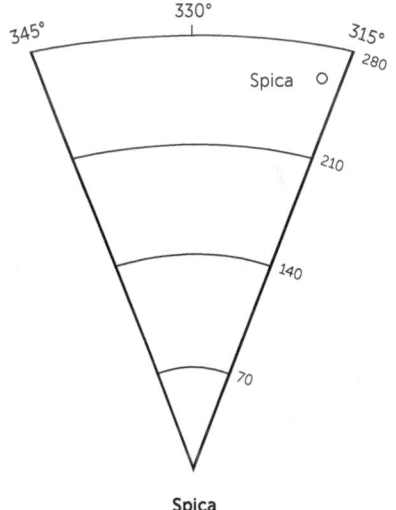

Spica
318° N 51° 260 l.y.

Crux Section

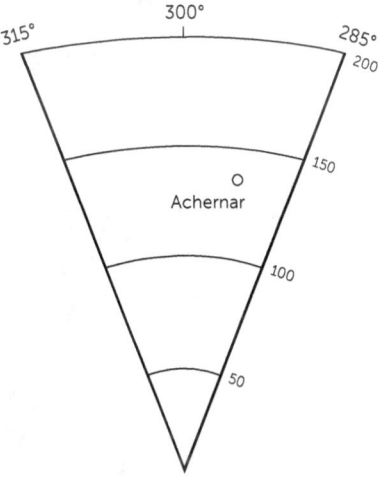

Achernar (A. Eri)
292° S57° 139 l.y. (a landmark)

Vela Section

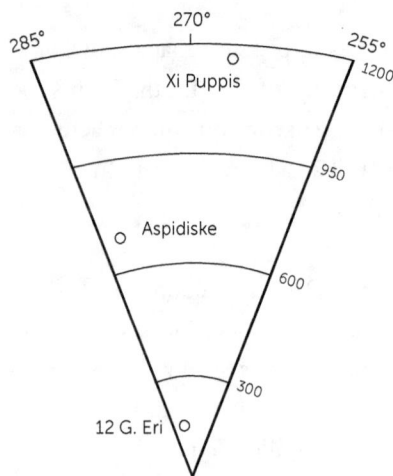

12 G. Eri
280°   S62°   154 l.y.   (Planet Skylark?)

Xi Puppis
266°   S8°   1200 l.y.

Aspidiske (I. Car)
280°   S15°   690 l.y.

Puppis Section

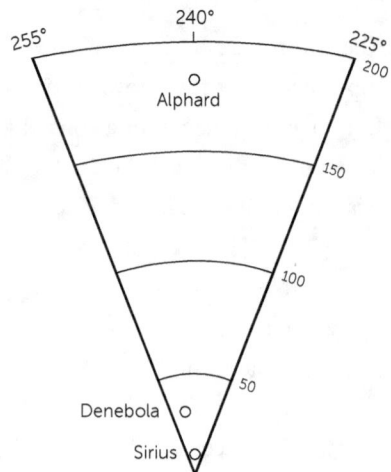

Sirius
228°   S8°   9 l.y.

Alphard (A. Hyd)
240°   N30°   177 l.y.   (planet Quantique)

Denebola (B. Leo)
252°   N73°   36 l.y.   (planet Terranova)

Monoceros Section

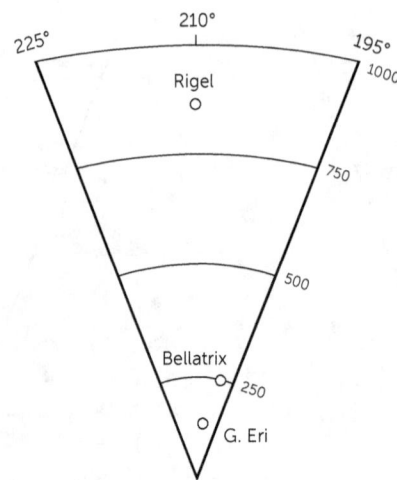

G. Eri
205°   S44°   150 l.y.   (planet Reis)

Rigel (B. Ori)
210°   S25°   860 l.y.   (Rigel Concourse)

Bellatrix (G. Ori)
198°   S16°   250 l.y.   (planet Tranque)

Auriga Section

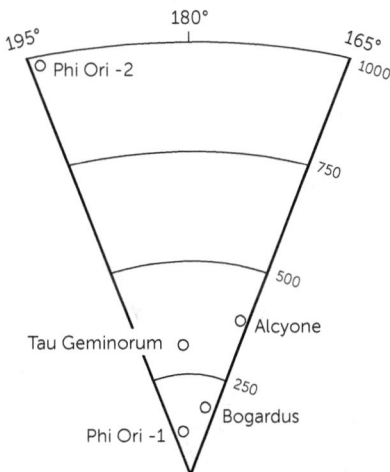

195° 180° 165°

○ Phi Ori -2

1000

750

500

Tau Geminorum ○

○ Alcyone

250

○ Bogardus

Phi Ori -1 ○

Alcyone (E. Tau)
165° S22° 370 l.y.

Bogardus (Theta Aur)
175° N8° 166 l.y. (planet Bogardus)

Phi Ori-1
195° S22° 120 l.y. (planet Zade)

Phi Ori-2
195° S22° 1000 l.y. (planet Zade)

Tau Geminorum
187° N17° 320 l.y. (planet Valhalla)

Perseus Section

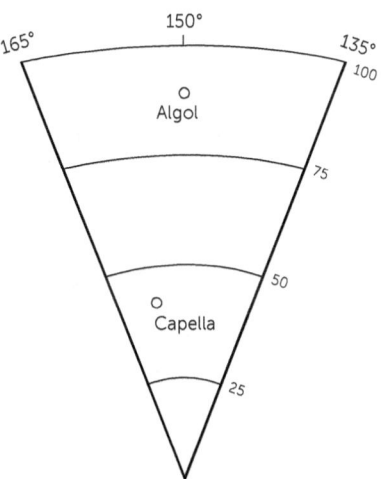

165° 150° 135°

○ Algol

100

75

○ Capella

50

25

Algol
150° S15° 93 l.y. (as a landmark)

Capella
160° N4° 42 l.y.

Casseiopeia Section

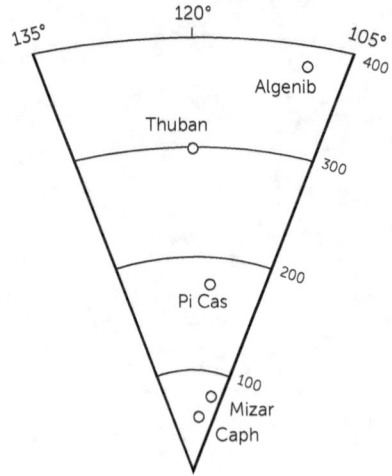

Algenib (G. Reg)
110°   S45°   390 l.y.

Caph (B. Cas)
118°   S40°   55 l.y.

Pi Cas
120°   S15°   174 l.y.

Mizar
112°   N63°   83 l.y.   (planet Mizar IV)

Thuban (A. Dra)
120°   N50°   300 l.y.

Cygnus Section

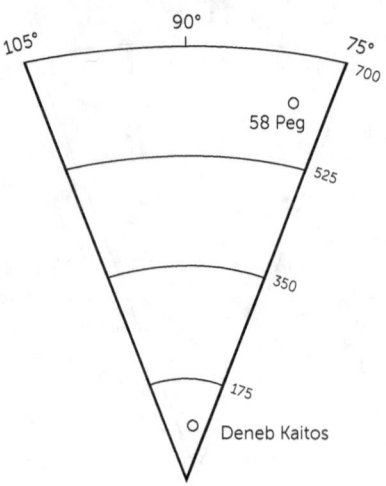

Deneb Kaitos (B. Cet)
85°   S80°   96 l.y.   (planet Amenaro)

58 Peg
80°   S48°   619 l.y.   (planet Rhea?)

Vulpecula Section

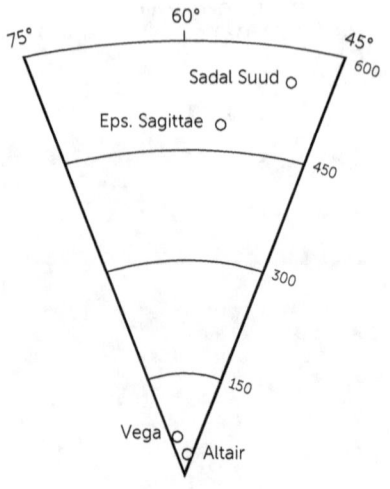

Altair
48°   S9°   17 l.y.

Vega
68°   N20°   25 l.y.

Eps. Sagittae
55°   473 l.y.   (planet Verlaren)

Sadal Suud (B. Aqr)
50°   S40°   550 l.y.

Aquila Section

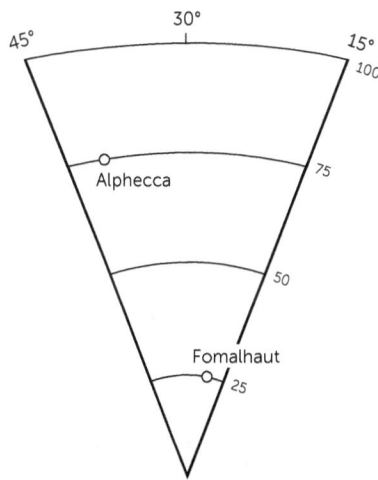

Alphecca (A. CrB)
42° N54° 75 l.y. (planet Amenaro)

Fomalhaut
21° S66° 25 l.y. (planet Sandusk)

Sagittarius Section

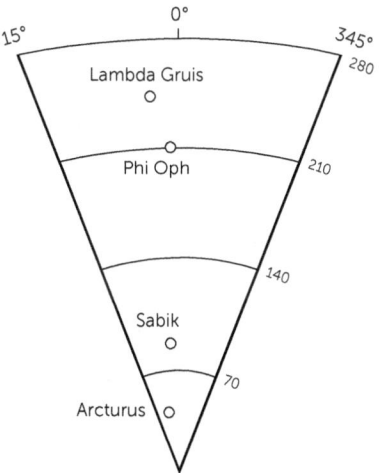

Arcturus
12° N68° 37 l.y.

Sabik (Eta Oph)
7° N14° 90 l.y. (planet Vadilov)

Phi Oph
1° N21° 210 l.y. (planet Sarkovy)

Lambda Gruis
2° S55° 242 l.y. (planet Ghnarumen)

APPENDICES

SPACESHIPS

ARIEL a comparatively inexpensive space yacht of the Gaean Reach, a modification of the ancient Model 11-B Locator, it sells for about 20,000 sols (NL 5.2). The same craft by different builders is the Cody Extensor and the Spadway Hermit. Having a broad beam, it is fifty feet long.

ARMINTOR STARSKIP an elegant starship of the Oikumene (KM 8).

BAUMUR ANDROMEDA a good ship for trips within the Sirneste Cluster (PL 10).

CD 16 a ship type of the Oikumene (SK 9).

DEVAUNT CADET PLANET-JUMPER a low-priced spaceyacht of the Gaean Reach, costing SVU 9,800 (MT 11).

DISTIS IMPERATRIX a model of the Oikumene, made by Distis Spaceship Corporation (PL 2).

DISTIS PHARAON an Oikumene model (PL 2). A large ship.

FANTAMIC FLITTERWING in the Oikumene, a space cruiser with a small cargo hatch and accomedations for four (F 7; BD 1). It is larger than the Distis Pharaon, more comfortable than the Armintor Starskip.

FLECANPRAUN MARK SIX a type of small spaceship in the Gaean Reach (Th 4.3).

FORTUNATUS NINE a brand of space yacht in the Gaean Reach, worth 65,000 sols (Th 3.2). It is 65 feet long, containing a large saloon, galley, three double cabins, storeroom and utility room on the top deck, with the engine room, dynamics, crew's quarters, and further storage and utility rooms on the lower deck. Its squat oversize sponsons are integral with the hull (Th 4.1).

GULSCHWANG 19 a Gaean Reach space yacht worth over two million sols (NL 5.2).

MAGELLANIC WANDERER a Gaean Reach vessel with accommodation for 16 plus a crew of six, valued at SVU 327,000 (MT 11).

MODEL 9B LOCATOR a standard scoutship for a planetary locator of the Oikumene, it is a thirty-foot cylinder with the bare essentials. There are three sections: the first is the bridge, the midsection is the living quarters; and aft is the energy block, the Jarnell Intersplit, and further storage (SK 1).

PARABOLA a ship type of the Oikumene (SK 9).

SISSLE WANDERWAY a ship type of the Oikumene (BD 11).

TELEFLO a Gaean Reach starship (MT 11). Accommodation for six plus a crew of two, all for SVU 18,500.

NOTES ON TRAVEL TIMES

In the Oikumene, a trip from Vega to Marhab in the middle reaches of Aries (BD 1) seems to take less than a day, perhaps even less than eight hours. Other trips are measured in days, up to a week. The journey from Rigel to the Beyond takes some days, with perhaps another day or two to get to Thumbnail Gulch (SK 10). The voyage from Thumbnail Gulch to Teehalt's Planet goes beyond "the first few days" (SK 11), and a week feels about right.

In *Son of the Tree* the trip from Juction to Ballenkarch is seven days (ST 10), and since Junction is equidistant from Ballenkarch, Kyril, and Mangtsee, then travel to them would be the same.

In the Gaean Reach, it appears that the voyage from Mariah to Fluter takes a few days (Lu 3.4).

In *The Five Gold Bands*, the trip from Mirach to Delta Trianguli using the Langtry space-drive is said to take either a day (FGB 13), or a few days (FGB 14). Current calculations put the distance between these two real stars at 166 l.y. Covering that in 24 hours would be a rate of nearly 7 l.y. per hour; in 48 hours that would be 3.5 l.y. per hour; in 72 hours that would be 2.3 l.y. per hour.

In *Space Opera*, the trip from Old Earth to Sirius Planet takes about a week, though it might be as short as 4 days. The distance to Sirius is 8.4 l.y., so the rate appears to be about 1 l.y. per day, or 2 l.y. per day as a maximum.

In the Planet of Adventure series, it is a given that the distance from Old Earth to Tschai is 212 l.y. On planning his return, Adam Reith expresses calculations about the time: "In one month [the ship will be ready]…In another month you will be repaid" (D 14). Reith might be bluffing here, but if taken at face value it implies a round-trip time of one Tschai month, which is assumed to be roughly equal to an Earth month, wherein the 212 l.y. distance would take two weeks to cross. This would be a rate of about 15 l.y. per day, or .6 l.y. per hour.

A very precise figure is given for travel in the Commonwealth: the fastest a ship can go is 42.5 l.y. per day (SAN).

In the Tellurian Empire, it takes about four days to go from Earth to the edge of the Clantlalan System, and seven days to go beyond the edge of explored space (WT 1).

SPORTS

HADAUL OF DAR SAI

Darsh men enjoy playing in and betting on "hadaul," a game of physical prowess and cunning played upon a prepared surface having three concentric circles and a pedestal.

The pedestal stands with the prize money at the center of a maroon disk. This disk has a radius of four to eight feet. Around this disk are three concentric rings, each ten feet wide: first yellow, then green, and finally blue. The area beyond the blue ring is called Limbo.

The typical number of "roblers," or players, is from four to twelve. At the start, all roblers take position on the yellow ring and are considered "yellow roblers." When the game begins, they attempt to eject others into the green roble through wrestling, butting, tripping, and hurdling. Once thrust or thrown into the green, a robler becomes "green" and may not return to yellow. Greens work to eject others into blue. A yellow robler may cross into green and blue and then return to yellow; in a similar way, a green robler may cross into blue and return.

Generally the goal is to have a single yellow robler as the only robler remaining, and he wins the pot. Sometimes the game ends with one yellow, one green, and one blue, whereupon they split the prize 3:2:1. At that point green or blue may wager new sums equal to the yellow prize and by this means again become yellow. The process continues until a single robler remains to claim the entire prize, or the roblers come to some compromise.

Conspiracy is a big part of the game. Before the game starts the various roblers form alliances of offense or defense, which may or may not be honored. Tricks, crafty betrayal, and duplicity are all considered natural techniques of the game. To be chased three times around the ring means automatic ejection into the next roble.

Victories can be challenged by anyone who can put up a challenge stake. This results in a special duel, where the challenged one gets to choose the weapons used.

HUSSADE OF THE ALASTOR CLUSTER

Hussade is a contact sport wherein two opposing teams strive to denude the enemy princess while protecting their own.

The hussade field is a gridiron of "runs" (also called "ways") and "laterals" above a tank of water four feet deep. The runs are nine feet apart, the laterals twelve feet. Trapezes permit the players to swing sideways from run to run, but not from lateral to lateral. The central moat is eight feet wide and can be passed at either end, at the center, or jumped if the player is sufficiently agile. The "home" tanks at either end of the field flank the platform on which stands the sheirl.

Players buff or body-block opposing players into the tanks, but may not use their hands to push, pull, hold, or tackle.

The captain of each team carries the "hange"—a bulb on a three-foot pedestal. When the light glows the captain may not be attacked, nor may he attack. When he moves six feet from the hange, or when he lifts the hange to shift his position, the light goes dead; he may then attack and be attacked. An extremely strong captain may almost ignore his hange; a captain less able stations himself on a key junction, which he is then able to protect by virtue of his impregnability within the area of the live hange.

The sheirl stands on her platform at the end of the field between the home tanks. She wears a white gown with a gold ring at the front. The enemy players seek to lay hold of this gold ring; a single pull denudes the sheirl. The dignity of the sheirl may be ransomed by her captain for five hundred ozols, a thousand, two thousand, or higher, in accordance with a prearranged schedule. (Tr 7)

A team has two Wings (Left and Right), two Strikes, two Rovers, four Guards, one Captain, and one sheirl. There are also five reserves, making a total of sixteen men and a virginal young woman. ("Forwards" seem to number four, probably wings and strikes together.) Each player is outfitted with a team uniform and helmet, as well as a "buff," a three-foot padded club.

HUSSADE TERMS

Gialospan—literally "girl-denuder."
Isthoune—exalted pride and confidence.
Kercha'an—effort conducing to superhuman feats of strength and will.
Mana—the emotion that compels heroes to reckless feats.
Sashei—that wild and gallant élan which inspires a team to transcend its theoretical limitations.

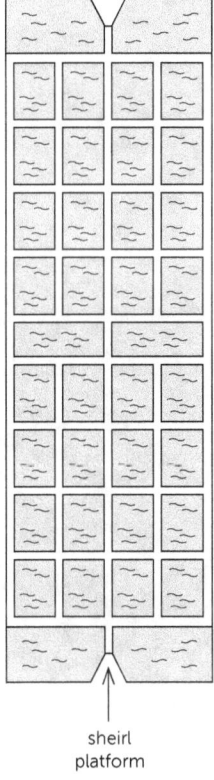

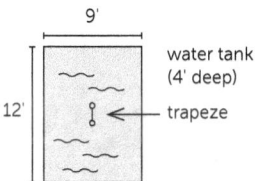

9'

water tank
(4' deep)

12'

trapeze

**Hussade Field
or Gridiron**

sheirl
platform

TENTATIVE UNIFIED TIMELINE

A few words on this assemblage are in order. Obviously the Oikumene and the Gaean Reach are set in their time periods, with the Gaean Reach being a successor to the Oikumene. Beyond that, there are few markers to be found within a text to suggest where it might be located in history, but one is a passing reference to recorded history on Earth, which allows such titles as *Space Opera* and the Planet of Adventure series to be fitted in.

Year	Event
-9.3 meg	On Tschai Pnume history begins around the time of the Shivvan invasion.
-? meg	On Tschai the alien Gjee invade.
- ? meg	On Tschai the alien Fesa invade, expunging the Gjee.
- ? meg	On Tschai the alien Hsi invade (Pn 12).
-129,100	On Tschai the Old Chasch arrive (CC 4).
-115,500	On Tschai the Blue Chasch arrive and fight the Old Chasch.
-99,000	On Earth the Star Kings visit, take Neanderthals (SK 8).
-75,500	On Tschai the Dirdir arrive and fight the Chasch (CC 4). The Dirdir subsequently bring proto-Mongol humans (CC 2).
-49,000	On Earth the Star Kings drop off "Cro-Magnons" (SK 8).
-27,500	On Earth, prehistoric humans develop stardrive, go to planet Yan (SO 10).
-22,200	On Tschai the emergence of steppe humans; the Old Chasch enter senescence; the Dirdir bring proto-Caucasians (CC 4).
-8500	On Tschai the Wankh arrive and fight the Dirdir.
-5500	Earth history begins at Sumer (3500 BC).
0	Year AD 2000 (Old Style): Space Age begins (SK 7).
150	On Earth, the California Tri-centenial (MMU).
?	*The Five Gold Bands* (Langtry: early stardrive).

300	On Earth, Yan dissidents crash on Isle of Man, then flee to Wales to escape persecution (SO 10).
400	"Sjambak" takes place, referencing 5,000 years from Mohenjo-Daro, which was established in 2600 BC. Probable setting of the Commonwealth era.
500	*Space Opera* takes place (ancient Athens restored; 6000 years of human history; interstellar travel at 1 light year per day).
500+	*Big Planet* takes place (Earth colony 500 years).

THE OIKUMENE

Year	Event
500	Planet Thamber colonized (KM 9).
800	Bissom's End colonized.
993	The Oikumene has over ninety inhabited planets (SK 3).
1000	Planet Krokinole referenced (SK 1).
1020 c.	Jarnell Intersplit discovered; star travel much faster.
?	"The Moon Moth" takes place.
1028	Valhalla referenced (SK 3).
1075	Birth of the Interworld Police Coordination Company, or IPCC (SK 3).
1292	*Popular Handbook to the Planets* (edition 303) published (SK 4).
1325	Planet Thamber's "Time of Great Heroes."
1404	Article on Brinktown (SK 2).
1479	Smade colonizes Smade's Planet (SK 1).
1499	Demon Princes raid on Mount Pleasant (SK 10).
1500	Conclave of Demon Princes at Smade's Planet, where they divide the Beyond amongst themselves (SK 10); the Texahoma Riots occur on Old Earth (KM 5). Article on Star Kings (SK 9).
1502	Address by the Institute (SK 8).
1509	Article on trade (KM 1).
1520	Article on city Rath Eileann of Aloysius (F 2).
1521	Televised debate between Institute and Planned Progress League (PL 10, 11). Article on perfume (KM 11).
1523	*Cosmopolis* article on Smade of Smade's Planet (SK 1).
1524	*Star King* takes place (SK 1).
1525	*Popular Handbook to the Planets* (edition 348) published (PL 1); *The Killing Machine* takes place (KM I).
1526	*Palace of Love* takes place (PL 1).
1527	*The Face* takes place (assumed).
1528	*The Book of Dreams* takes place (assumed).
1530+	*The Demon Princes* by Caril Carphen published.

(THE MIDDLE MILLENNIA)

Year	Event
1500	"Emphyrio" legend written (E 19).
1500	"The Men of the Ten Books" takes place (7,000 years of human history).
1500+	*Showboat World* takes place, referencing play "Emphyrio" (ShW 1).
3500+	*Emphyrio* takes place 2,000 years after writing of Emphyrio legend, at a time when Halma has been a human colony for 3,500 years (E 20).
4300	On Tschai the human Golden Yao of Cath transmit on interstellar radio and are crushed (CC 4).
4500	On Tschai the Planet of Adventure series takes place, with reference to 10,000 years of human history (CC 2).
5000+	*Languages of Pao* takes place, where Pao has been colonized for 5,000 years (LP 18).
9000+	Durdane series, where Durdane has been colonized for 9,000 years (An 9).

THE GAEAN REACH

Year	Event
25,000	Planet Fader colonized (NL). Safronilla located by Wilbur Wailey. Mariah located by Abel Mirklint.
27,000	On Fader the High Era begins.
28,000	On Mariah, fourteen alien statues are discovered. On Fader, the Bad Times period begins.
29,000	Count Sarbert founds the Naturalist Society (EOE 6). Wyst is colonized. On Maz, a "Hate" war forms the Steppe of Long Bones.
29,800	The Submission Treaties of Koryphon (GPr prologue).
30,000	Alastor Cluster novels, the Cadwal Chronicles, *The Gray Prince*, *Maske: Thaery*, *Night Lamp*, and *Galactic Effectuator* all take place.

(POST-GAEAN PERIOD)

Year	Event
?	*To Live Forever* takes place.
?	*The Dragon Masters* takes place 812 years after the War of Ten Stars and the collapse of the Human Empire.
?	*The Last Castle* takes place 3,700 years after the Six Star War leaves Earth fallow for 3,000 years.

SOURCE TEXTS AND THEIR PRIMARY PLANETS

"Abercrombie Station"—mention of Bella's Pride, Codiron, and Pest-hole.

"Assault on a City"—mention of Caph III and Rampold.

Big Planet—Big Planet; Index.

The Blue World—Blue World and New Ossining.

The Cadwal Chronicles—Cadwal, Natrice, Old Earth, Soum, and Tassadero.

"Cholwell's Chickens"—Alnitak Five, Beau Aire, Codiron, Emeraud, and Puskolith.

"Coup de Grâce"—Hub; Cambyses, Duax, Hecate, Journey's End, Padme, S-Cha-6.

"Crusade to Maxus"—Exar, Fell, and Maxus.

Demon Princes series—Aloysius, Alphanor, Bethune Preserve, Boniface, Cuthbert, Dar Sai, Euville, Ghnarumen, Krokinole, Methel, Mizar VI, Mt. Pleasant, New Concept, Old Earth, Olliphane, Quantique, Sarkovy, Sasani, and Thamber.

"The Devil on Salvation Bluff"—Glory.

"The Dogtown Tourist Agency"— Delta Rasalhague and Maz; Arbello, Arbonetta, Cicely, Dys, Fallorne, Fanuche, Glamfyre, Lusbarren, Marmonfyre, Tamar, and Varsilla.

The Dragon Masters—Aerlith and Coralyne.

Durdane Series—Durdane and Kahei.

Emphyrio—Damar, Halma, Maastricht, and Earth.

The Five Gold Bands—Akhabats, Alpheratz A and B, Badau, Canopus Four, Delta Trianguli, Deneb Ten, Green-Rassins, Koto, Loristan, Maeve, New Hellas, Novo Mundo, Shaul, Spade-Ace.

"Freitzke's Turn"—Gietersmond, Thesse, and Wittenmond; Alpheratz VI, Cambiasq, Dashbourne Planet, Lutus, Neroli, Skalkemond, and Wicker.

"The Gift of Gab"—Sabria; Alkaid Two and Starholme.

Gold and Iron—Magarak; Bakaima, Baliberos, Brengastel, Calbys, Eifal, Jeol, Klau Empire, Koethena, Lekthwa, Lenau, Perdu, Pterni, Purloppat.

"Golden Girl"—Ghh'lekthwa.

The Gray Prince—Koryphon; Alcide, Darybant, Diamantha, Pharistane, and Tanquil.

"The House Lords"—BGD 1169.

The Houses of Iszm—Iszm; Capella XII, Cleo 8, Eta Scorpionis, Fei, Martinon's Fort, Mazen, Monago, Starholme.

"The Howling Bounders"—Naos V, Naos VI.

"The King of Thieves"—Moritaba; Almanatz, Archaemandryx, Judith IV, Medellin, New Acquitain, Ophir.

The Languages of Pao—Batmarsh, Breakness, Hallowmede, Journal, Mercantil, Pao, Polensis, and Vale.

The Last Castle—Old Earth; mention of Albireo VII, Altair, Etamin Nine, and Spica X.

"The Man from Zodiac"—Ethelrinda Cordas; Lucia Cordas.

Marune: Alastor 933—Bruse-Tansel, Marune, and Numenes; Azulias, Blazon, Dadarnisse Junction, Deulle, Douaune, Haune, Imber, Tsambara, and Xampias.

Maske: Thaery—Eiselbar and Maske; Bossom's World, Diosophede, Dwet, Phrist, Quincunx, and Zalmyre.

"Masquerade on Dicantropus"—Dicantropus; Clave II and Thuban XIV.

"The Men of the Ten Books"—Arcturus Five and Haven.

"Meet Miss Universe"—Achernar, Alphard, Alschain, Aries 44R951, Arneb, Aspidiske, Chromosphoro, Claverops, Conexxa, Delta Corvi, Deserta Delicta, Gamma Grus, Gomeisa, Grglash, Jheripur, Kaus Australis, Mel, Persigian, Sadal Suud, Shaula, Theta Piscium, TIX, Veidranu, and Vindemiatrix.

"The Miracle Workers"—Pangborn.

"The Moon Moth"—Sirene.

"The New Prime"—Belotsi, Chankozar, Old Earth, Praesepe Three, and Staff.

Night Lamp—Camberwell, Fader, Gallingale, and Nilo-May.

"Nopalgarth"—Gher, Ixax, and Nopalgarth.

"Phalid's Fate"— Phalid; Bao, Coralangan, Kordecker 343, and Lojuk.

"The Planet of the Black Dust"—Planet of the Black Dust; Gavnad, McVann's Star.

Ports of Call series—Alcydon, Arcturus Legend, Blenkinsop, Derard, Dimmick, Ergard, Fiametta, Fluter, Kodaira, Komard, Kyril, Mariah, Naharius, Numoy, Sarbane, Scropus, Star Home, Taubry, Terce, Vermazen.

"The Potters of Firsk"—Channel Planet and Firsk.

"Sabotage on Sulfur Planet"—Rho Ophiuchus IV.

"Sanatoris Short-cut"—Fan, Sanatoris Beta.

"Shape-Up"—Fenn and Procrustes.

"Sjambak"—Cirgamesç; Alphard IX, Gropus, Nekkar IV, Riker's Planet.

Son of the Tree—Kyril, Junction, Ballenkarch; Ardemizian, Beland, Castlegran, Cil, Frums, Giansar, Jamivetta, Jonapah, Kelce, Mangste, Panapol, Perkins, Polaris, Rosalinda, Thombol, Thuban Nine, Xenchoy, Zarjus.

"The Spa of the Stars"—Kolama.

Space Opera—Capella IV, Hydra GRA 4442, Old Earth, Procyon planet, Rlaru, Sirius Planet, and Zade.

"The Sub-standard Sardines"—Chandaria; Mugh, Pandora, Rhodope, Sirius Five, Thaddeus XII.

"Sulwen's Planet"—Sulwen's Planet.

"The Temple of Han"—Magra Taratempos.

"Three-legged Joe"—Odfars and Old Earth.

"To Be or Not to C or to D"—Jexjeka; Alpheratz IX, Azul, Exigencia, Fan, Formaferra, Gamma Scorpionis, Gengillee, Hephaestos, Julian Wolters IV, Lennox IV, Mallard 42, New Sudan, Omicron Ceti III, Rhodope, Thaluri Second.

Trullion: Alastor 2262—Trullion; Balmath, Ellent, Gray World, Green Star, Illucante, Maranian, Rhamnotis, Rufous Planet, and Triskelion.

"Ullward's Retreat"—Old Earth, Mail's Planet.

"The Unspeakable McInch"—Sclerotto Planet; 1012 Aurigae, Carnegie Twelve, Portmar's Planet, Sirius Five.

"When Five Moons Rise"—Magda.

"Winner Lose All"—Alexander, Antaeus, Coralasan, and Procyon B.

"The World Between"—New Earth; Alvan, Blue Star, Canopus, Copenhag, Graemer System, Kay System, and Maraplexa.

"The World Thinker"—Laoome's world; Clantlalan System, Fan, Hycithil, Starlen.

Wyst: Alastor 1716—Numenes, Wyst, and Zeck; Arcady, Kandaspe, Lambeter, and Pharis.

CONCERNING THE RIGEL CONCOURSE

There is a vexing problem regarding the Rigel Concourse.

At first glance it looks simple and straightforward—twenty-six habitable planets, each granted a name beginning with a different letter of the alphabet. A series from Alphanor to Zacaranda.

FIRST MODEL

Orbit	Planet
1-6	Inner Belt
8	Alphanor
14	Krokinole
19	Olliphane

However, after the six incandescent worlds of the inner belt, comes Alphanor, the first of the Concourse, as planet eight rather than seven. So which letter comes before "A"?

The pattern is further scrambled. If the planets were alphabetical from Alphanor to Krokinole, then Krokinole would be planet 18, yet Krokinole is given as planet 14. If the planets were in alphabetical order from Krokinole to Olliphane, then Olliphane would be planet 18, but it is given as planet 19.

Olliphane is "Located close at the outer edge of the Habitable Zone" (SK 5). This is rather alarming, since "O" is scarcely half-way through the alphabet, and even "planet 19" implies that there are more habitable planets to follow (exactly how many depends on where the counting starts). For if one counts the Rigal Concourse Number as beginning with the planet before Alphanor, still the Olliphane planet . . .

SECOND MODEL

Orbit	Planet	RC#
1-6	Inner Belt	
7		1
8	Alphanor	2
14	Krokinole	12
19	Olliphane	15

In fact, this is wrong—the Inner Belt is not part of the Concourse, which is made up of 26 habitable planets. Furthermore, "orbit number" is not the same as "planet number." So there are seven planets of the Concourse before Alphanor, presumably being warmer worlds. Alphanor, Krokinole, and Olliphane represent the middle worlds, and after Olliphane the seven remaining worlds get cooler.

To be perfectly clear, the planets have names assigned by letters from the alphabet but they are not in alphabetical order.

THIRD MODEL

RC#	Planet
1	(warmest)
8	Alphanor
14	Krokinole
19	Olliphane
26	(coldest)

As to the 26 names themselves, they seem to fall into five different groups:

Group	Names and Notes
Whimsical (11)	Barleycorn, Image, Krokinole (a game), Nowhere, Quinine (medicine), Somewhere, Tantamount, Unicorn, Walpurgis (May Day), Xion (a Chinese city), and Zacaranda.
Names (8)	Alphanor (surname), Chrysanthe (girl's name "marigold"), Diogenes, Fiame (surname), Hardacres (surname Hardacre), Olliphane (surname "elephant"), Pilgham (surname), and Valisande (a princess name in Vance's mystery *The View from Chickweed's Window*).
Legendary Lands (3)	Elfland, Lyonnesse, and Ys.
Biblical (2)	Goshen (place in Egypt where the Hebrews lived) and Jezebel.
Islands (2)	Madagascar and Raratonga.

NOTES ON THE MODES OR PHASES OF MARUNE

One of the most intriguing details regarding the modes or phases of Marune is given when the hotel employee refers to a specific mode: "isp 25 of the Third Cycle" (Ma 4). In the context, this sounds like a day within a month or an hour within a week; in essence, the "Third Cycle" is a block of time wherein the mode "isp" has repeated 25 times. Modes might all last a specific amount of time, perhaps six to eight hours. A later statement seems to peg it at six hours, when, "after six hours of aud," mirk comes (Ma 10). In an attempt to narrow it down, I trace the text.

On the day of the crime, it was aud at the beginning of the adventure in town (Ma 5). After the hero's memory was erased, it was umber (Ma 13). Transitions such as this tell us little about the duration of a mode.

The first days of investigation give the most complete sequences of modes in the text. The time is isp when the hero arrives at the spaceport, located a mile from Old Town (Ma 4). He takes a bus, gets off at the hotel of the second stop, eats lunch, and lingers. (Presumably this takes up about one hour, but there is no clue as to how far advanced the mode of isp was when he started.)

As he walks back to the spaceport, the mode rowan begins. He gets to the spaceport and interviews an employee, then turns around and walks to Old Town, going to the hotel of the third bus stop. The mode changes to green rowan. (The first walk probably took 20 minutes; the interview another 20 minutes; and the second walk 30 minutes, so it would appear that rowan lasted a bit more than one hour.)

The hero enters the hotel, interviews an employee there, and emerges into the mode umber. (This makes it plain that green rowan lasted only twenty or thirty minutes.) In umber he walks slowly through Old Town, taking in the sights. He does not have another meal, which is significant in that meal-tracking is another way to judge time. The hero returns to his hotel and sleeps for an unspecified period of time, to rise at the breakfast gong.

When the hero sets out from the hotel it is half-aud (Ma 5), then comes isp (Ma 6), and finally umber (Ma 6). The hero sleeps seven hours. The mode is aud about to become chill isp (Ma 6), implying that the hero slept through all of aud, at least, and perhaps another phase as well. In the course of his activities chill isp is followed by umber (Ma 7) and green rowan (Ma 7). His companion retires to sleep at half-aud (Ma 8), and the next mode is lorn umber (Ma 8).

If a mode lasts for six hours, then the hero was awake for 24 hours in that final sequence of chill isp, umber, green rowan, and half-aud. This seems fitting, yet the text suggests that green rowan, the one time we saw it, lasted a mere half hour. If the average duration of a mode is six hours, then some must be longer. While it is not certain that each mode has a fixed duration, here is a list of observed cases:

- *Isp*—more than one hour.
- *Rowan*—a bit over one hour.
- *Green rowan*—a half-hour.
- *Aud*—six hours.

These are four of the ten modes, and for them to have an average of six hours each, isp would have to be 16.5 hours, which seems too long for a mode. If isp and the other six unknown modes average 7.5 hours each, then the average for all ten modes would be six hours.

Which brings us back to "isp 25 of the Third Cycle." Now that we have a sense of how long a phase lasts, we can make calculations of differing scales. Twenty-five times six hours equals 150 hours. This is a large block of time: a week is 168 consecutive hours; a month is 672 consecutive hours; a season is 2016 consecutive hours. Isp is one of ten modes, but we don't know how often they repeat: some modes may repeat more often than others, and mirk definitely comes only once a month. So the Third Cycle cannot be a week, nor is it likely to be a month, but it might be a season.

Approaching modes can be seen in the sky, hence the term "low aud" for when aud is about to change to umber. In addition, the castles can tell time in advance. The hero calls for a meeting in 20 hours, but his servant tells him that will be "in the middle of mirk" (Ma 9). At another point, the hero says, "Let us adjourn until next aud" (Ma 12).

In any event, the text gives several clear examples showing modes lasting from 30 minutes to six hours. This goes a long way toward defining the wonderfully mysterious modes of Marune.

ITINERARIES

A

1. Vermazen	8. Fluter	15. Kyril
2. Dimmick	9. Star Home	16. Naharius
3. Taubry	10. Blenkinsop	17. Taubry
4. Scropus	11. Mirsten	18. Alcydon
5. Terce	12. Avente	19. Vermazen
6. Fiametta	13. Archimbal	
7. Mariah	14. Fluter	

B

1. Delta Rasalhague	2. Maz

C

1. Bruse-Tansel	3. Imber	5. Tsambara
2. Deulle	4. Numenes	6. Marune

D

1. Earth	5. Yan
2. Sirius Planet	6. Rlaru
3. Zade	7. Earth
4. Skylark	

E

1. Earth
2. Altair
3. Vega
4. Giansar
5. Polaris
6. Thuban
7. Ardemizian
8. Panapol
9. Rosalinda
10. Jamivetta
11. Kyril
12. Junction
13. Ballenkarch

F

1. Smade's Planet
2. Euville
3. Alphanor
4. Olliphane
5. Alphanor
6. Thumbnail Gulch
7. Teehalt's Planet

G

1. Welters
2. Sussea
3. Fluter
4. New Hope
5. Kyril
6. Lavendry

SUBJECTIVE LISTINGS

AROMAPHILIC WORLDS: Marune, Quantique.

AUTARCHIES: Alastor Cluster, Pao, Shant (Durdane).

BALKANIZED WORLDS: Aerlith, Big Planet, Durdane, Thamber, Tschai.

BORDER WORLDS: Maz, Tschai.

CHAOTIC DAYLIGHT: Glory, Marune.

CHROMOPHILIC WORLDS: Durdane, Eiselbar.

CRIMINAL COLONIES: Blue World, Brinktown.

HOUSEBOAT WORLDS: Sirene, Trullion, Zeck.

LOW-METAL WORLDS: Big Planet, Blue World, Durdane.

LOST/HIDDEN WORLDS: Blue World, Fader, Thamber, Tschai?

MUSICAL WORLDS: Camberwell, Eiselbar, Sirene.

NATURE PRESERVES: Bethune Preserve, Cadwal, Maske, Methel.

NON-MUSICAL WORLDS: Marune, Wyst.

PRISON WORLDS: Interchange, New Ossining, Scropus, Skylark.

PRISON WORLDS (FORMER): Boniface.

REFUGE WORLDS: Aerlith, Pangborn.

SHIPWRECK COLONIES: Blue World, Haven.

STATUS SOCIETIES: Cadwal, Gallingale, Sirene.

WELFARE STATES: Halma, Wyst.

SECONDARY TEXTS

Dibon-Smith, Richard. *StarList 2000*. New York: John Wiley & Sons, 1992.

Mead, David G. *An Encyclopedia of Jack Vance, 20th-Century Science Fiction Writer*. New York: The Edwin Mellen Press, 2002.

Parmentier, Gregg (ed.). *The Vance Phile No. 1-5*. Iowa City, Iowa: Parm Press, 1993-1995.

Pasachoff, Jay M. and Donald H. Menzel. *A Field Guide to the Stars and Planets (Third Edition)*. Boston: Houghton Mifflin, 1992.

Rawlins, Jack. *Demon Prince: the Dissonant Worlds of Jack Vance*. San Bernardino, California: Borgo Press, 1986.

Stephensen-Payne, Phil and Gordon Benson, Jr. *Jack Vance: A Fantasmic Imagination: Galactic Central Volume 28 (Second Revised Edition)*. Albuquerque, New Mexico: Galactic Central, 1990.

Temianka, Dan. *The Jack Vance Lexicon*. San Bernardino, California: Borgo Press, 1995.

Underwood, Tim and Chuck Miller (editors). *Jack Vance (Writers of the 21st Century Series)*. New York: Taplinger Publishing Company, 1980.

LIST OF REAL STARS

1. Achernar
2. Adhil
3. Albireo
4. Alcyone
5. Algenib
6. Alkaid
7. Almach
8. Alnitak
9. Alphard
10. Alphecca
11. Alpheratz
12. Alschain
13. Altair
14. Arcturus
15. Arneb
16. Aspidiske
17. Baten Kaitos
18. Bellatrix
19. Beta Trianguli (see CONEXXA)
20. Bogardus
21. Canopus
22. Capella
23. Caph
24. Cassiopeia 993:9—as Cassiopeia HD 993.
25. Chandaria—probably orbits CD -23° 1799, a class K7 V star.
26. Delta Aquilae
27. Delta Corvi
28. Delta Trianguli
29. Deneb
30. Deneb Kaitos
31. Denebola
32. Epsilon Sagittae
33. Eta Cassiopeiae (see GRGLASH)
34. Eta Piscium
35. Eta Scorpii
36. Etamin
37. Fomalhaut
38. Gamma Eridani
39. Gamma Gruis
40. Gamma Scorpii
41. Giansar
42. Gomeisa
43. Kaus Australis

LINKAGES BETWEEN TEXTS

Granted that the Oikumene era is confined to the Demon Princes series (five books), and the Gaean Reach epoch is fairly well demarked (12 books at least), and these series are linked through the IPCC, the presence of Ambeules on Old Earth, and other details.

THE OIKUMENE
The Demon Princes (5 volumes)

GAEAN REACH EPOCH
The Cadwal Chronicles (3 volumes)
Galactic Effectuator (DTA and FT)
The Gray Prince
Marune: Alastor 933
Maske: Thaery
Night Lamp
Ports of Call (2 volumes)
Trullion: Alastor 2262
Wyst: Alastor 1716

In addition there are subtle links between other texts.

TELLURIAN STORIES
"The World Thinker"
"Planet of the Black Dust"
"Phalid's Fate"

Through mention of the Clantlalan System, "The World Thinker" is connected to "Planet of the Black Dust." "Phalid's Fate" is also Tellurian (PF 4). "The World Thinker" mentions Fan, the Pleasure Planet, which is part of the Commonwealth. So these three stories are set in the Tellurian Empire, seemingly a precursor to the Commonwealth.

> **COMMONWEALTH STORIES**
> Magnus Ridolph stories (10)
> "Sjambak"
> "Masquerade on Dicantropus"

The ten Magnus Ridolph stories are set in the Commonwealth. The story "Sjambak" seems set in the Commonwealth because of reference to the monetary unit "munit" (used in the Commonwealth) as well as mention of "the Earth Commonwealth." "Sjambak" also gives a rough date of AD 2,400 for the setting (5,000 years after Mohenjo-daro). "Masquerade on Dicantropus" mentions "munits," suggesting that it, too, is a Commonwealth story.

> **BIG EMPHYRIO**
> *Big Planet*
> *Emphyrio*
> *Showboat World*

Big Planet is succeeded by *Showboat World,* making a two-book series. In the first chapter of *Showboat World* there is mention of the play "Emphyrio," which forms a strong bond to the novel *Emphyrio.*

> **HOUSE OF GAB**
> *The Houses of Iszm*
> "Gift of Gab"

The Houses of Iszm and "Gift of Gab" share mention of an inhabited world "Starholme."

> **THE OIKUMENE EXPANDED**
> The Demon Princes (5 volumes)
> "The Moon Moth"
> *The Blue World*

Additions to the Oikumene: In *The Killing Machine,* the information on the cosmopolitan world Quantique contains this tidbit: "The people of this fantastic and beautiful land are as sensitive to odors as the Sirenese are to music" (KM 11). This refers to the planet Sirene as featured in the story "The Moon Moth." Within that tale, there is no mention of the Oikumene, there is only brief allusion to "the Home Planets." So the Home Planets would seem to be a precursor to the Oikumene, or a translation of the term.

The Blue World makes brief reference to "the Home Worlds," which forms a tenuous connection to the Home Planets of "The Moon Moth." It also mentions "New Ossining" as a penal planet, which forms a link to the city New Ossining on Olliphane of the Rigel Concourse. Both of these details hint that *The Blue World* is set around the time of the Oikumene.

EXPANDED GAEAN REACH
The Cadwal Chronicles (3 vol.)
Galactic Effectuator
The Gray Prince
The Languages of Pao
Marune: Alastor 933
Maske: Thaery
Night Lamp
Ports of Call (2 volumes)
Trullion: Alastor 2262
Wyst: Alastor 1716

Adding to the Gaean Reach: The Gaean Reach novel *Night Lamp* gives fleeting reference to a group of stars called "Polymarks" (NL 12.6), which seems a close fit to the Polymark Cluster featured so prominently in *The Languages of Pao*.

LEKTHWAN
"The Golden Girl"
Gold and Iron

"The Golden Girl" and *Gold and Iron* share golden humans called Lekthwans. "Golden Girl" is a first contact story; *Gold and Iron* comes later, when the Lekthwans have established a presence on Earth that is a challenge of wonders and a threat of overwhelming human civilization. The heroine of "Golden Girl" is named Lurulu, and she suffers deep melancholy from being stranded on Earth; this links up to the novel *Lurulu,* sequel to *Ports of Call,* where the term "lurulu" is defined as "something lost and unknown which we seek to discover" (POC epilogue); one character later says "it is like hope, or a wistful longing, more real than a dream" (Lu 12.6).

www.ingramcontent.com/pod-product-compliance
Lightning Source LLC
Chambersburg PA
CBHW051650260626
47170CB00004B/1427